SEALS

Again Tynan used his binoculars. From the new angle, he could see a couple of more hootches constructed along the lines of the first few he had seen. In the center were several cages, but there was no movement in them. Then, as the rising sun turned night into morning, Tynan spotted the men locked in the cages. He put the binoculars on them. Each was shackled, the leg irons leading from raw, bleeding ankles to posts driven into the ground. Each wore rags that once had been uniforms. They were tired-looking, skinny men, who moved slowly, as if they were very old. They were sick and mistreated

BREAKOUT!

SEALS

#5

BREAKOUT!

STEVE MACKENZIE

AVON
PUBLISHERS OF BARD, CAMELOT, DISCUS AND FLARE BOOKS

SEALS #5: BREAKOUT! is an original publication of Avon Books. This work has never before appeared in book form. This work is a novel. Any similarity to actual persons or events is purely coincidental.

AVON BOOKS
A division of
The Hearst Corporation
105 Madison Avenue
New York, New York 10016

First Avon Books Printing: January 1988

AVON TRADEMARK REG. U.S. PAT. OFF. AND IN OTHER COUNTRIES, MARCA REGISTRADA, HECHO EN U.S.A.

Printed in the U.S.A.

K-R 10 9 8 7 6 5 4 3 2 1

1

The United States Navy SWIFT boat, its engines idling, drifted toward the lush green vegetation at the river's edge. SEAL Lieutenant Mark Tynan stood on the bow and watched as the boat touched the soft, wet mud of the bank. As it stopped, he leaped forward into the thick grass and then crouched, waiting. A moment later four more men joined him and the engines of the boat reversed, pulling it back into the deeper water of the middle of the stream.

Without a word, the men fanned out until each of them was barely visible in the gray-white of the dawn's mist. They were ghostlike shapes filtering through the trees and between the bushes. The low rumble of the boat's engines changed to a full-throttled roar as the coxswain spun the wheel and took the boat upriver to complete its mission.

As the sound from the SWIFT boat dissipated, Tynan stood up and moved cautiously into the dense vegetation. He halted inside the trees, one knee on the moist ground. Slowly, he used his eyes to search the jungle in front of him. He listened to the noise made by the animals: the monkeys in the trees above him, the birds flying overhead. Around him, all seemed to be normal and natural.

He waited as one of the men, Thomas Jones, a tall, thin, blond man now dressed in camouflage fatigues with a face smeared by camo paint and a mottled, green, dark brown, and black scarf tied around his head to hide his hair, moved forward to take the point. He hesitated, listening, and touched his face with his hand, looking at the sweat on it. He then eased into the dense bush carefully, watching for the thorns of a wait-a-minute vine, and for the thin, black wires that marked a Vietcong booby trap. He stopped once, bent low, and touched the ground with his fingers. The backs of his hands were smeared with camo paint, too. Once he was into the tropical flora, where the sunlight was filtered by triple canopy, Jones would be nearly impossible to see, unless he was moving.

Tynan slipped in behind him, following in his footsteps. He didn't have to look to know that the rest of the team had followed suit. As he moved deeper into the jungle, he eased his hand along the stock of his CAR-15, his thumb resting on the selector switch.

They moved slowly, placing each foot carefully to avoid making any noise. Jones ducked under a low-hanging branch that dripped water, then dodged to his right. Tynan ducked under and then turned to the left, sliding along the edge of a path, using the bushes and ferns to conceal himself from any Vietcong who might be around.

He glanced to the rear and could see one of the others, but not the last two. As he turned, Jones ducked around another bush and disappeared into the darkness. Tynan followed and spotted him crouched at the edge of a small clearing. Sunlight was filtering in, but the sun wasn't high enough to have burned off the morning mist.

Jones raised an eyebrow in question.

Tynan shrugged and then pointed to the left, indicating for Jones to skirt the edge of the clearing. Jones got up and stepped to his left. His head swiveled right and left as he searched for the enemy that could now be hiding anywhere. He kept moving without making a sound.

Tynan lifted his shoulder and touched his forehead, wiping the sweat from his face. He swallowed, realizing that he was thirsty but couldn't take a drink. Wasted motion would only make him thirstier and might call attention to him. He would have to ignore his thirst until they took a break. He felt the perspiration drip down his back and trickle along his sides. Even without the sun overhead, it was hot in the jungle. The humidity hung in the air like old laundry.

They continued to move as the sun rose higher and the jungle began to steam. There was a dank odor in the air like a basement that had been closed throughout the summer and it seemed that there was a curtain of mist drifting upward. The moisture was thick, highlighted by the sun's rays in the rare places where light could punch through the triple canopy. As they brushed against the leaves and branches of the plants, water dripping from the upper levels splattered them.

After an hour, Tynan called a halt. No one spoke as they spread into a loose circle, each man able to see the man on either side of him. Half of the men kept a watch while the others drank from their canteens. Tynan drank deeply and gratefully. The water tasted of hot plastic but it was just what he needed. He poured the last of his water from his first canteen on the camouflaged scarf and draped it over his head. If the air hadn't been so heavy with humidity, it would have cooled him as it evaporated.

Without a word, the men formed up again after a fifteen-minute rest, Jones taking point again. He avoided one trail that wasn't much more than a footpath hidden under the trees and looked like a long, narrow, green tunnel. After he crossed it, he halted and pointed back to it once. As Tynan approached, he understood the signal: there were several footprints in the soft, moist soil.

Stopping long enough to examine one closely, Tynan knew immediately that the prints had been left by the enemy: the prints were made by sandals cut from tire tread. The feeling of apprehension that had bothered him from the moment he entered the jungle now had some justification. Although the soil was soft, the markings were still sharp. There was water beginning to seep into the bottom of the prints, which weren't more than an hour old.

As soon as Tynan crossed the trail, he found Jones crouched there waiting. He put his lips close to Tynan's ear and said, "Those guys are moving south."

Tynan nodded his agreement. He glanced into the jungle, trying to see beyond the thick bushes and the tall trees, the hanging vines and the broad leaves, wondering about the enemy soldiers.

"Do we take them?"

The last thing Tynan wanted was to leave a known enemy unit behind him on his line of communication. Militarily, it was bad to bypass the enemy without determining his size and mission. He looked at Jones's eyes and saw them sparkling in the dull, half-light and knew that Jones wanted to take them. Tynan nodded once and pointed.

Jones came up off the ground and stepped back to the trail. He then moved off it so that he was paralleling it, but concealed by the verdant vegetation. He stayed in the deep shadows, planning each step before he made it. Then he began to move faster, sliding around the bushes and the trees, stopping occasionally to check the trail.

Their overall progress was slow. They couldn't make noise and they were traveling over rough terrain. But they kept at it, listening for the enemy, watching for him.

It was nearly noon when Jones froze. He didn't move for a full minute. The patrol behind him did the same, waiting until Jones signaled them to take cover. Tynan glided closer to him and was going to ask what the problem was when he saw it for himself. Spread out along the side of the trail were several of the Vietcong. Four of them were visible, each wearing black pajamas, a pith helmet, and a chest pouch for the banana clips for his weapon. It was obvious that they were waiting to ambush somebody.

Tynan touched Jones on the shoulder, then nodded toward the rear. Quietly, they fell back, watching their step now that they knew the enemy was so close.

They reached the main part of their patrol. Tynan crouched, one knee on the damp ground. He leaned forward, an elbow on his other knee, and closed his eyes to think. For a moment the only thing he could focus on were the heat and the humidity, so thick that he could almost taste them. He was slightly light-headed and wanted only to stop this nonsense and go home. Drink a cold beer and go to sleep.

He opened his eyes and stared at the bright green leaf of a plant. A patch of sunlight had set it glowing emerald. Then he looked into the faces of the team crouched around him waiting for instructions. Even though they were all within inches of him, their camouflage paint made them hard to see.

"Okay," he whispered, "we've an enemy ambush laid out in front of us. I can't leave it here on our lines of communication, so we need to take it out."

There were slight nods from two of the men. The others sat quietly waiting.

"We'll infiltrate slowly and kill them one by one. I don't want any shooting if we can help it."

There wasn't anything more to say about it. Each man knew what his job would be. They would slip up behind the V.C. set in the ambush and kill them one by one using their knives. If they did it right, they wouldn't alert the men who were left alive and the SEALS would then have a chance to kill them all.

Tynan nodded and turned. He began the slow process of working his way through the thickly packed undergrowth. Tynan avoided the thorn-covered vines that could rip his uniform. When he was near the rear of the ambush, he dropped to the ground, crawling forward. It was slow, hot work. He had to be careful not to make a sound and give himself away, yet he didn't want to move so slowly that he couldn't get into position. Tynan tried not to think about what was going to happen. He kept his eyes moving until he spotted the back of one of the enemy soldiers. Then he froze, waiting.

The rest of the team slipped through the jungle as silently as Tynan had. The little noise they made was masked by a light breeze rattling through the tops of the trees, and the monkeys leaping in the high branches.

Tynan waited a full fifteen minutes so that the team would have a chance to infiltrate. When the time had passed, Tynan slung his CAR-15, and drew his knife. He rose up on his hands and knees. He came to his feet, crouched low, and moved forward. With one hand on the ground to balance himself, Tynan stopped right behind the enemy soldier. In one fluid movement, his hand snaked out, grabbing the man. With his hand clamped over the enemy's mouth and nose, he dragged him back. The V.C. lost his balance and fell. As his hand reached up in surprise, Tynan cut the man's throat with one quick movement. Blood spurted, spattering the plants like a light rain. He kicked out a foot as he died. He'd had no chance to warn his fellows.

Tynan laid the body down and turned. To his right, he saw Jones dispatch his enemy soldier. Blood squirted in a crimson fountain, and there was a quiet groan as the man died. He never knew what hit him.

Jones rolled the body to the left, under the leaves of a large bush. He moved forward then, as if taking the ambush position the dead man had held.

When the long axis of the ambush had been quietly eliminated, Tynan slipped to the rear and moved up on the anchor leg. With a single, bold move, Tynan took out the last of the enemy. The man had stood up in panic, calling softly to his men as if sensing that something had happened. Tynan stepped behind him, slapped a hand over the man's mouth, and jammed the knife upward over the kidney so that it pierced a lung and the heart. As the man sagged, dying, Tynan cut his throat. There was the stench of bowel as the man's blood splashed over Tynan's hand with an odor of hot copper.

As he dropped the dead man, there was a rustling up the trail. Tynan crouched and stared into the dense undergrowth. Jones slipped closer and said quietly, "Someone's coming."

"Who?"

"Patrol. Maybe ten, twelve of them. NVA."

"Then we take them too. L-shaped ambush. Grenade blast signals the beginning of the ambush. No one fires until the grenade detonates."

"Aye, aye."

Tynan took the anchor position of the ambush, the body of the dead man by his knee. After taking his CAR-15 from his shoulder and checking the safety, he set the butt of his weapon on the ground, and pulled out a grenade. He jerked the pin free, and set it on the ground where he could find it again if he wanted it. Then he froze, waiting for the enemy to enter the killing zone of the ambush.

They would now control the operation, although they didn't know it.

Tynan wasn't happy about it. The circumstances had forced him to accept an ambush site selected by someone else. Selected by an enemy officer who might have had the training to do the job right. Obviously it wasn't a good site because they had found it from the rear. Given the chance, he would have inspected the site to make sure that there was a clear killing field and that there was no easy way to get behind it. He could see that the trail was five or six feet wide and the bush on the opposite side was thin, but it wasn't a perfect site.

From the far side of the ambush came a bubbling laugh and then an order in quiet Vietnamese. To Tynan, it meant that the enemy was at home in the area. They felt safe moving in the daylight and ignored normal patrol discipline.

The first of the enemy soldiers appeared. This was not another V.C. unit, but hard-core NVA. These were soldiers in khaki uniforms, pith helmets, and boots. Each carried an AK-47, each wore a chest pouch for the spare magazines, and each wore a woven pistol belt closed with a buckle with a red star. They had more equipment than a normal V.C. unit. They carried canteens, knives, and even entrenching tools.

And they weren't paying attention to what they were doing. They were strolling through the jungle like it was a walk in the park. A couple of them held their weapons in their hands, but the rest had slung them or had balanced them on their shoulders. They weren't even watching the trail, searching for booby traps. It meant they knew that there were none scattered around.

As the point men, two NVA soldiers walking side by side and chatting quietly, approached, Tynan let the safety spoon on the grenade fly. He counted to two and threw the grenade over the heads of the two men. When it detonated with a dull explosion in the middle of the jungle that destroyed the silence, the other men opened fire. There was a crash as the SEALS began pouring rounds into the enemy patrol.

Tynan snatched his weapon, leveled it, and pulled the trigger. He turned it sideways and dragged it from right to left, holding the trigger down and raking the trail and the jungle vegetation.

The first of the point men went down with bullets in his stomach and chest. The second tried to dive for cover, but Tynan hit him in the side. He shrieked in pain as he fell, then pulled at his weapon, trying to get it around. But Tynan didn't give him a chance: he fired again, the rounds slamming into the man's shoulder and head, blowing his helmet off.

As the second point man collapsed to the ground, his blood pooling around his head, the firing died. The enemy patrol was scattered on the trail—a shattered group of men with white bone gleaming through the holes blown in their twisted and broken bodies. The air was heavy with the odor of copper and the stench of bowel.

Tynan waited for a moment, watching the dead. None of them moved. The damage that he could see—gaping wounds in their sides and chests, limbs severed from bodies, and pools of blood staining the rotting jungle vegetation—said that all the enemy soldiers were dead.

Cautiously, Tynan stood up, his weapon pointed at the dead men. He crouched near the first man, pushed the AK-47 out of the man's reach, and was tempted to put his fingers against the bloody throat to feel for a pulse. The wounds to the stomach had ripped it open, exposing the intestines. The man's unseeing eyes stared at the ground. It was obvious that the man was dead but Tynan still felt like searching for signs of life.

Instead of checking for a pulse, however, Tynan began to search the pockets. He found nothing of interest there. He poked through the rucksack but there were no papers or documents. Just the man's supplies, spare clothes, and personal items.

The whole team moved out to the trail with the exception of the men providing security. They searched the dead, taking the weapons and ammo and any documents they could find. As the men moved among the dead, the buzzing of flies started up. Hundreds of them began to appear out of the jungle, covering the wounds of the dead. The noise of them grew until it sounded like buzz saws in the distance.

When the team had finished searching the bodies, they withdrew quickly. Tynan put Jones on point and then dropped back as the rear guard. He had hesitated for a few moments over the direction, wondering if the mission had been compromised by the enemy. The mere fact that they stumbled over the NVA so quickly answered one of the questions. Now, with two patrols missing, how would the enemy react? Tynan decided that he didn't want to hang around to find out.

He gave Jones a compass direction and told him to stop at the river's edge. Once there, they would slide along it for a click or so, looking for a place where the PBR could get in close to pick them up. The last thing he wanted to do was use the place where they had landed. That was the way men got killed. Taking the easy way out and refusing to give the enemy credit for brains.

They moved through the jungle, dodging the clearings and the sun, until late in the afternoon. Then, soaked with sweat and breathing heavily because of the heat and humidity, Tynan called a halt. He spread the men out in a loose circle, each man keeping an eye on the men to his right and left, and gave everyone a chance to eat, drink, and rest.

As the sun touched the horizon, they moved out again, this time keeping at it until they could smell the river in the distance. Again they halted for the night—half the men on alert while the other half slept, rotating the duty every two hours so that no one man pulled too much of the guard.

Tynan took the first watch. He lay on his stomach, the rotting vegetation and the moist earth only inches from his nose. He kept his eyes moving, trying to memorize the locations of the bushes and trees, looking for the movement that would give away the enemy patrols. But he saw and heard nothing other than the nocturnal animals and natural sounds, and finally turned the watch over to the next man.

Tynan rolled cautiously to his back. He stared upward but could see only a dark smear above him. The leaves and branches of the trees interwove into a thick canopy that blocked out the sky and stars. He stared upward anyway, listening to the quiet sounds of the jungle around him.

After what seemed to be only a few minutes, he felt someone touch his shoulder. He was awake immediately, his eyes searching the vegetation around him, knowing before he opened his eyes that it was one of his men. Without a word, he rolled over and moved into a position to watch for the enemy.

Just before dawn, Tynan moved to the radio and, using the agreed-on codes, he requested that the PBR come in to pick them up. He gave their coordinates and informed them that the shoreline was secure. Although there were enemy patrols in the vicinity, he had had no contact with the enemy for over twelve hours.

As dawn broke, with the monkeys screaming and the birds squawking, Tynan heard the rumble of the PBR's engines. In minutes, the men were on board and they were racing back down the river, heading for the closest base. Tynan checked his men, gathered the documents together, and then sat down to wait. The mission had been a success.

2

Lieutenant Mark Tynan sat in the office of Commander Richard Clafin. It was a rich office, decorated with watercolors by local artists, carpeting on the floor, and furniture shipped from the United States at great cost to the American taxpayers. Tynan sat on the couch of blue crushed velvet and wondered how much longer it would hold up in the tropical environment of South Vietnam. In fact, looking at the office, Tynan wasn't sure if Clafin was furnishing an office or a bordello. Everything seemed to be gaudy.

Tynan had been given little time to clean up after his patrol. The PBR had docked at a small base and then the SEALS been flown by Huey to the coast. Once there, Tynan had willingly surrendered his dirty, stained, and torn jungle fatigues for a new uniform. He had taken a shower, combed his hair, which was now longer than regulations allowed, and shaved everything but his mustache, which was something he had been cultivating for the last couple of months.

Tynan was a tall, thin man who was beginning to push thirty. He had hair that had been bleached by the sun, and his eyes were a light blue that looked as if they had been washed out by the same bright sun. His eyebrows were nearly nonexistent. Although he didn't look strong, he was wiry and had a strength that surprised a lot of people. His major attribute in combat was his quickness. If Vietnam had been the Old West, he would have been considered one of the fastest guns alive.

Clafin sat behind his mahogany desk, writing on a stack of papers in a thick file folder. He had glanced up when Tynan entered and then waved the younger officer to a chair as he bent back to his work. He wrote on a dozen sheets of paper, dumped them into the out basket, and then slowly put the cap back on his pen.

Tynan wasn't sure that he cared for the trick. He was tired of men who demanded that he meet them immediately and then kept him waiting while they finished some vital piece of paperwork. It was a tactic designed to show who was important and who wasn't.

However, Clafin ruined the effect by standing and coming around his desk, smiling as if genuinely happy to see him. He was a short man who was slightly stooped over. He had a large face with a big nose and bushy eyebrows. It made it hard to remember any of the other features. He stopped in front of Tynan and held out a hand.

"I'm sorry about that," he said, nodding toward the paperwork. "I hate it and if I don't get it finished when I have a run at it, I let it slide too long and my yeoman has to finish it for me. That's not fair to him although he keeps telling me he doesn't mind. I guess it's better than being in the field."

Tynan stood and shook hands. "I understand, Commander."

"Please, sit down." He stepped back and leaned against the edge of his desk. "Now, I'm going to give you a quick briefing, off the record, that deals with the information your team brought in this morning. Then we'll have to decide what you're going to do with it."

"Then you've gotten the documents translated?" Tynan rocked back and crossed his legs.

"Yes. Or rather enough of them." He glanced around, as if looking for spies, and then said, "What you located—or rather, what you captured—are the interrogation records of a number of prisoners of war."

"Oh," Tynan said noncommittally.

Again Clafin looked for the hidden spies. "Now, the important thing is not that we've got these papers, but that they give us enough information that we can almost pinpoint the camp."

Tynan sat quietly for a moment, letting the information sink in. Then he felt the excitement claw at his stomach. He wanted to shout, but contained himself. He wanted to run, wanted to do something to take the edge off. Trying to keep the excitement from his voice, he asked, "And you want me to go back and try to free the prisoners?"

Clafin smiled and said, "If it wouldn't be too much trouble."

Tynan wanted to stand and pace. His mind raced as he thought his way through the information that he had been given, slight as it was. To Clafin he said, "We ambushed two enemy patrols in the space of about five minutes. When they learn about that, they're going to move that camp because they'll assume that we're on to them."

"Yes, that was what Intelligence claimed. Said that as soon as it was discovered that the patrol with the records was ambushed and that the documents are missing, Charlie would move the camp. Take him a day to do it. Maybe less."

"Then we've got to get back in there. Today. Now," responded Tynan.

Clafin reached around and touched a button on his desk. In the outer office there was a faint buzz. Before anyone could react, Clafin said, "I was hoping you'd say that."

The door opened and the yeoman stood there. "Yes, Commander?"

"I want you to get my jeep ready and alert Captain Avery that I will be along in twenty minutes with the man. He'll understand."

"Aye, aye, sir."

As the yeoman disappeared, Clafin asked, "How long to get your team back together?"

Tynan pulled the sleeve of his uniform out of the way and studied his watch. He grinned and said, "Well, if they haven't had time to drink themselves into oblivion by now, probably thirty minutes. That's if they stopped to drink and didn't hitch a ride into Saigon."

"Drinking this early?"

"Commander, when you've been awake virtually all night, then it's not early, but very late, so I would think that they're drinking."

"Do what you can and then report to me here and we'll drive over to the conference room. If there's anyone you can't find, spread the word and have him meet us there. Questions?"

"Just one: Is the information being taken at face value?"

"That will be answered later, but right now, the answer is yes. Everyone who's looked at it thinks that it's good. The enemy gains nothing by it, and there was no way for them to predict that your team would be in the area."

It was closer to an hour before Tynan and his team arrived at the conference room. It was a small room with cinder-block walls and an old table in the center. There were a couple ashtrays on the table, which was scarred by multiple cigarette burns. There was a rattling of air conditioning somewhere overhead. The walls, painted a light green, were bare. The floor was polished concrete without a rug or mat. There was no obvious screen or projector.

Tynan sat at one end of the table, the members of his team near him. All were wearing new fatigues, though they were already sweat-stained and smelling of cigarette smoke. Tynan had found them grouped together in an N.C.O. club sucking down beer and smoking cigarettes and talking about sleeping. They had decided that they didn't want the girls to show up until they all had managed to catch ten hours of sleep.

Jones leaned across John Mathis, a tall, stocky man with jet black hair and skin scarred by acne, and said, "What's all this about, Skipper?"

"Just be patient and you'll find out."

"Well, sir, I've got a couple of things I'd like to do, one of them being sleep."

"Tommy always wants to sleep," said Mathis. "You'd think that's the only thing to do."

"In Vietnam, the more you sleep, the shorter your tour. At least, it seems shorter."

"Knock it off," snapped Tynan.

Across from him sat Bill Callahan, who had black hair and a heavy beard that required shaving twice a day. He was medium height and had a barrel chest. Although Callahan looked muscle-bound, he had a deceptive quickness that made him very dangerous.

Callahan's favorite activity was describing his adventures with the ladies. Many sailors indulged in the game, but Callahan liked to go into great detail talking of kinky times. Tynan was never sure whether the tales were invention or if Callahan had actually indulged in the practices. Given the nature of the SEALS, anything seemed possible.

Next to him was Bruce James. Tynan had met the man only recently, just prior to the last mission. James was skinny, almost emaciated, with pasty skin that rejected the sun. The heavy camo paint he wore protected his skin from the tropical sun in the field and Tynan wondered if he stayed inside when they were at the camp.

James was a strange man. He looked on the verge of collapse, but could hump through the boonies all day without getting tired. He carried extra ammo because he had a pathological fear of running out while in a firefight.

At the base, he was quiet, usually refusing to join the men in their adventures in the various clubs. But in the field, he seemed to be a top-notch soldier.

The door to the conference room opened and Clafin stepped in. He moved back out of the way and said, "Room, attention."

The men got slowly to their feet. Mathis slouched as if to prove that he wasn't impressed. The rest of them stood straight, their hands at their sides.

Two more men entered. One of them was in fatigues that contained no insignia, the other wore a khaki uniform with shoulder boards showing the stripes of a captain.

"Be seated," said the captain. "Okay, Commander, let's get this show on the road."

"Aye, aye, sir." He went over the information he had discussed with Tynan so that his men would understand the nature of the mission, explaining the location of the enemy camp in relation to the river and the roads and the American bases in the area. He had a map but there was no easel to hold it and no bulletin board to tack it to. He spread it on the table and pointed out the important terrain features. He then showed them where the camp was located, based on the information they had pulled from the documents.

"Wouldn't it be easier to land in there with a flight of Huey helicopters and a bunch of people from the Air-cav?" asked Mathis.

"Might be easier, but I'm not sure how effective," said Clafin. "The Air-cav couldn't sneak in. Charlie'd hear them coming from a mile out and either move the camp before the troopers could land and get there, or kill them and exfiltrate themselves."

"So this is another sneak-and-peak operation," said Tynan.

"Not sneak and peak," said the captain. "We want you to go in and check out the situation carefully. Then you're to free those men and get them out."

Tynan looked at the men with him. Four men, three of whom he didn't know that well. He would have preferred to assemble a team from the people he had worked with for a while and then take them into the field for a training exercise. It wasn't that he thought them incompetent, it was that he didn't know them. Didn't know how they'd react in a tight situation.

"How long?"

The captain consulted some notes and said, "You're into the field at sunset. PBR to take you in and then you'll have to work your way to the camp. You'll have to recon and decide the best way to get our boys out."

Tynan shook his head. "Given what we know, I'd say that we'll need fifteen more men."

"And what do you base that on?" asked the captain.

"What Nick Rowe said after he escaped from the V.C. in the delta. There'll be between twenty and thirty guards around. They'll have an advantage in terrain and they don't have to be quiet. We slip up once, make one mistake, and the whole mission collapses."

"Then you'll have to be very careful," said the captain. He turned on Clafin and added, "Commander, I think you'll have to make the situation clear to Lieutenant Tynan."

Clafin sat down and pulled at the map. He twisted it around and studied it. Without looking up, he said, "The feeling is that you men here, because you've been in the area, will be familiar with the terrain so that Charlie loses that advantage. The feeling is that a few highly trained men should be able to handle the situation by themselves."

"But—" said Tynan.

"Lieutenant," said the captain, "there is no *but* here. Your orders are to go in. The PBR leaves this afternoon. Now, what do you need?"

Tynan stood and moved to Clafin. He glanced over his shoulder and looked at the map. There was a red mark where the enemy camp was supposed to be. From the river it was nine or ten clicks. Tynan had seen the jungle and knew that it would be difficult to move through it, especially at night, which was when he'd want to travel. They would have to stay away from the trails and the paths. It would take them all night to get near the camp and they would have to lay low during the day, scouting the situation before they moved on it.

"It'll be two days before we can do anything."

"Why's that?" demanded the captain.

"Take us all night to get to the camp, and then we'll want a chance to check it out before we move. We can't rush in there cold."

"Run it the way you think best, but this is your mission," said the captain. "I'll arrange to keep everyone else out of the area until you've had the opportunity to complete the mission. They'll be helicopters and Air-cav standing by to reinforce and assist in the extraction if you need them. We can probably have a fighter squadron on call if you think it'll help."

"Equipment," said Jones.

"You give me a list of everything you want and you'll have it inside of ten minutes."

Tynan nodded and said, "Jones, I want you and Callahan on the equipment. Intersquad radios for communications between us and a PRC-77 for commo with the rear. You'll also have to pick up the extra ammo, claymores and tripwire booby traps, grenades, and anything else you think we'll need."

"Aye, aye, sir."

"Captain," said Tynan, "I want the transport arranged now and I want helicopters standing by to extract us in case we step into it. I don't want to lose the team in the event that something goes wrong. If I ask for extraction, I don't want a lot of arguments."

"As the commander on the scene, you'll get whatever you want."

Tynan pulled up a chair and slipped into it. He leaned forward and yanked the map closer, checking the distances, the terrain, and the general location. He discovered that they were in range of two American fire-support bases and one that had been given to the Vietnamese. Army aviation units were handy. They could lend either slicks for the extraction or gunships for close air support. Fighters from Saigon and the carriers in the South China Sea were also available. Help was within minutes, if Tynan decided that he needed it.

He glanced at his watch and saw that it was early afternoon. Suddenly he was nearly overwhelmed by a sense of doom. Everyone was pushing this so fast that there was no time to sit back and check for holes in the plan. It was just go, go, go, until the mission had taken on a life of its own and there was no one around to say, "Stop!"

"If there is nothing else," said Tynan, "I'd like to get my people out of here."

"I'd like you to remain behind," said the captain. "The rest can go if they'll remember that we can't discuss this outside the confines of this room."

"We know that," said Jones. "We've been around long enough to know better."

"Then you're dismissed."

Tynan turned in the chair and said, "Mathis, I want you to arrange for the C-rations and other supplies. Check the medical and first aid kits. Draw anything that you think we're going to need."

"Boots?" asked Callahan.

"If you want to break them in on patrol, go right ahead. Personally I'll keep the old ones," Tynan said.

"Maybe when we get back."

Jones moved to the door of the conference room and stopped. He looked at the other men and then at Tynan. "Anything else, Skipper?"

"No, I think that about covers it. If you don't see me before eighteen hundred, I'll meet you at the dock with the equipment."

"Aye, aye, sir."

When the men were gone, the captain leaned on the table so that he was closer to Tynan. He waited until Tynan looked at him and then said stonily, "I want it understood that you're to either rescue the men or . . . kill them. If you can't free them, they must *not* survive."

"What?"

"Lieutenant, there are things going on behind the scenes that you don't know about and don't have to know about. People in Paris talking peace while the war rages. Threats have been made. One of them is that maybe all our men won't be returned when the deal is finally cut."

Tynan sat back and stared at the captain. "I'm afraid that I don't understand."

"We are trying to negotiate a peace here without having established a clear victory. We keep fighting with one hand tied behind us. We pull our punches." He waved a hand to hold off the protest. "No, I don't understand it, but I know that you've seen it. Bombing of the north with the targets carefully selected to inflict some damage, but not the total saturation bombing that helped end the war in Europe. Our obeying, for the most part, the neutrality of the neighboring countries while the enemy ignores that."

"Or the war of terror waged on the civilians by the Vietcong and the NVA," said Tynan.

"Exactly. Now, it has been suggested that the NVA and the National Liberation Front will not agree to return of prisoners of war without some concessions from our side. Given the political climate, I think that our side will cave in."

"Yeah," said Tynan. "That's kind of the impression that we all have."

"Now we have the opportunity to send a message to the enemy and their friends in Paris. We know where some of our men are being held. We send in a rescue team, no holds barred. We either get them out alive or end the problem altogether."

Tynan just stared in disbelief. "You want us to eliminate the enemy, kill as many of them as we can?" he finally asked.

"A massacre would be nice. Kill them all, take no prisoners. You kill every swinging dick. Chase them into the bush to kill them if you have to, but make every effort to kill them."

"I understand."

"I want that camp eliminated. Once that has been accomplished, I want photos of it. I want pictures of the dead men and the burning camp."

"We have no one on the team who—"

"You don't worry about that. I have a man who will be going with you to document the raid."

"Now, wait a minute. I can't be saddled with some guy who is unfamiliar with the bush. He'll slow us down and he'll make noise."

"That is not your concern. The man is well trained and he'll hang with you. Don't worry about that. His job is to document the mission and that's his only job. It'll leave you free to accomplish what you have to do."

Tynan sat quietly thinking about it. The last thing he wanted was another man he didn't know. One who hadn't been through the Special Forces courses that he and his men had attended. Someone who hadn't spent the time in the bush that he had. Another unknown quantity who could screw up the mission without knowing it.

"We could assign someone to use the camera," offered Tynan. "One of my men."

"No, Lieutenant. You'll need all your men for the combat portion of the mission. It'll be better for us to give you one more man."

"But, Captain, we'll be moving through the bush and—"

"The point is not open for debate. You'll take our man in so that he can provide the documentation."

Finally he nodded. "Aye, aye."

"And remember, if you can't free the prisoners, kill them! You have to understand that. We have to prove to the enemy that we'll kill our own men before we'll allow them to be held as hostages. It'll give us the upper hand in the negotiations if the enemy knows that we'll kill our soldiers rather than allow them to be held."

"Jesus Christ," said Tynan.

"Exactly."

"There is one final complication," said the captain. He rubbed his face and then stared at his hand. "If you get into it, you'll have to get yourself out of it. I don't want you calling on those fire-support bases and fighter squadrons or army aviation."

"Then why in the hell would you organize that?" asked Tynan incredulously.

"Show, for the men. This has got to be a clandestine mission from start to finish. If it fails, and there is no record of it, then we can pretend that it never happened. You start calling in artillery and army aviation and air force fighter squadrons, the whole plan collapses."

Tynan shook his head. "You're beginning to sound like those politicians you were talking about. Here's a mission. Okay, a tough one, but one we can handle. Then we're handed a fucking list of restrictions that make completion impossible."

The captain turned in his chair and looked at the floor. "That's the nature of the war. It's not a war for warriors but one for politicians. That's why you have so many restrictions. It's something that the civilians and the newspaper reporters don't understand."

Tynan studied the map intently for a moment and then said, "If there is nothing else, I think that I'll get going. Before someone thinks of something else for us."

The captain held out his hand. "I understand your anger, Lieutenant, but the restrictions can't be helped. I can wish you good luck and let you know that the PBRs will be standing by. All you have to do is get to the river."

"Okay," said Tynan. He stood and added, "I don't like this at all, but I'll do my best."

"I know you will. Good luck."

"Thanks."

3

With all the briefings and coordination that was necessary, Tynan didn't manage to get away until it was time to head for the docks. Clafin drove him across the base, a neat camp with crushed gravel roads, whitewashed stones lining them, gray buildings with sandbag walls around them, and trim lawns. There were even brightly colored signs in front of the buildings, making it easier for visitors and the Vietcong, if they happened to attack. Sailors stood to the side of some of the buildings watering the lawns in the late afternoon sun.

As they passed all that, Tynan shook his head. They were supposed to be in a war zone, but the navy refused to believe it. They ran everything like they did their bases in the United States and their ships at sea. They ignored the enemy and the possibility of rocket or mortar attacks. They never left their base, simply pretended the war didn't exist.

Tynan just shrugged as they pulled up to the docks. He hopped out of the jeep and wiped a hand over his face. He was getting tired already. Up most of the night on patrol, then all day playing with the brass in briefings, and now back out into the bush. He took a deep breath and touched his lips with the back of his hand. At least it wasn't as hot as it had been. The sun was diving toward the horizon and the humidity seemed to have dried up. In fact, it was almost comfortable out. It was the first time that Tynan remembered being comfortable outside in Vietnam.

Clafin leaned across the jeep and said, "Good luck on this one."

"Thank you, sir."

"Remember what you've been told."

"Given the nature of the instructions, I doubt that I'll forget them."

Tynan turned and walked across the dry, red dirt. In front of him was a wooden dock and beyond that was the chocolate of the slow-moving river. The green of the jungle, where it hadn't been cut back by overzealous Seabees, reached out into the water, some of the leaves dipping into what little current there was. The sun, dropping for the horizon, sparkled and reflected from the river's surface, making it seem brighter than it was. Tynan put a hand up to shade his eyes as he stared at the scene spread out in front of him.

Jones and the rest of the team had the equipment laid out on the dock. Tynan moved among it, looking at it. He picked up one of the tiny radios for intersquad communications and then looked at Jones.

"These work?"

"Line of sight only, with a range of about two hundred meters in the open, more or less. In thick bush, if the antenna is pointed in the wrong direction, you won't be able to get the guy standing next to you."

"Yeah, well, we don't want too much range."

He moved off and crouched near a pile of C-rations. "What all you got here?"

"Just grabbed a couple of cartons and hauled them down," Mathis answered. "Threw out all the shit and kept the good stuff. Enough for a week in the bush."

Tynan stepped closer to the weapons and the ammo and examined them. There were claymore mines and hand grenades. There was enough spare ammo for the M16s to keep a platoon happy. There was a pistol for each man and ammo, but Tynan didn't think they'd be using the pistols on the mission. That didn't mean he wouldn't take them—only that he didn't think he'd need them.

"Claymores are good," Tynan said.

"Yes, sir," agreed Jones. "Wish we could carry a couple of dozen more."

"Okay." Tynan stood and turned, looking back toward the shore. The dirt road left the end of the dock and wound out of sight behind a long, low building with a tin roof that looked golden, and gray sides that were almost white. There were sandbags along the shoreside but not along the part that fronted the river. Tynan imagined that they figured a mortar or rocket dropping into the river wouldn't explode until it hit the bottom and the shrapnel would be absorbed by the water. He wasn't sure that he wanted to bet on it.

He moved to the edge of the dock so that he was in the shade created by the vegetation. It seemed almost cool there, but that had to be his imagination. Surveying the scene, he was once again overwhelmed by a feeling of dread. For an instant he was sure that he was going to die on the mission. He knew it as surely as he knew his own name. It was a scene out of a dozen bad movies. The man knowing he was going to die, so he wrote home telling everyone that he was going on a great adventure and wouldn't be returning. In the movies, the guy always died. In real life it rarely happened that way. He knew a dozen men who had been certain they were about to buy it and didn't. He shook himself and checked the gear one last time as he forced the thought from his mind.

As he stood up and checked his watch, he heard another jeep approaching. This one was driven by the captain from the briefing. Tynan still hadn't gotten his name. Sitting beside the captain was a skinny man in brand-new fatigues who looked as if he had arrived in Vietnam about an hour earlier.

When the jeep stopped and the man stood up, Tynan realized that nearly everyone he knew was skinny, with the exception of Callahan. It was from being in the bush for days on end, or weeks on end, from living as if each moment was the last, and from a lack of time to recover after each mission. No one had the chance to overeat, and if they'd got the chance, the food wasn't good enough for that.

The man came down to the dock, stopped, and stared. A moment later he moved toward Tynan and said, "Captain told me to introduce myself. I'm Webb."

Tynan held out a hand and asked, "What's your background, Webb?"

Webb shook hands and said, "I'm afraid it's classified."

"Classified or not, I need to know something about you," Tynan said.

"Well, let's just say that I've been to the survival schools in Panama and the Philippines and I know my way around the jungle."

"You spend any time in a combat environment?"

"As I said, sir, I've been to the various survival schools so that I don't think there'll be anything to surprise me. Good training."

Tynan nodded and turned. He sighed deeply. "Jones, let's get loaded up."

Once they had all shouldered their packs and checked their weapons, they moved along the dock. Tynan made sure that Webb took his share of the squad equipment and spare ammo. Although he tried to refuse a rifle, Tynan made him take it anyway. In a firefight sometimes it was just the ability to put out rounds that kept men alive.

At the PBR, they stopped until the coxswain told them to come on board. Then it was a problem of finding enough deck space to sit down. The boat was loaded with weapons. There were twin fifties and a 20 mm cannon along with an assortment of M60s and a couple of grenade launchers. Tynan wasn't sure there were enough men on the boat to man all the weapons the navy had hung on the PBR.

As soon as they were settled, the CPO in charge started the engines. There was a quiet rumbling in the rear and the deck seemed to vibrate with power. A couple of the crew tossed ropes ashore and they eased their way into the river.

At first they circled in the mouth of the river, burning up time. As the sun slid closer to the horizon, they turned upriver. Tynan sat watching the jungle slip by them: thick, dense jungle that lined the shores, some of the trees growing out of the water; jungle so thick that in places it seemed like a green wall with only a couple of bits of bright color spattered on it that was slowly turning black as the light from the setting sun faded.

When it was dark, Tynan closed his eyes and listened to the sound of the engines. From somewhere came the boom of artillery, and there was the occasional roar of a jet engine. All around was the popping of rotor blades as helicopters hovered over bits of jungle like giant birds of prey. But under all that, the quiet splashing of the water against the hull of the boat was somehow relaxing.

Tynan was on the edge of sleep when Jones touched him on the shoulder. Tynan snapped awake and stared into the darkness.

"Coxswain says we're getting close."

"You get the Dexedrine?"

"Sure did, Skipper."

Tynan held out a hand. "Give me a couple of them."

Jones opened his first aid kit and took out the Dexedrine. "You sure you need those?"

"Need has nothing to do with it."

At that moment, one of the crew stepped up and said, "We're getting close."

"Okay. I'd like for you to head upriver after you drop us off as a diversion."

"No problem, sir. Those are our orders. We're going to shoot up the shoreline in one of the free fire zones so that Charlie'll have something to watch." He grinned. "Nothing like a little target practice to brighten up the night."

Tynan nodded and stood. He reached down for his pack and slipped into it, adjusting the shoulder harness until it sat properly. That finished, he moved among his men, checking their equipment and packs, waiting for the sudden turn that would signal their approach to the shore.

As the boat turned, Tynan moved to the side to watch. With the sun gone, the shore was little more than a black smear just above the water. It looked like a solid black line, but as they approached it, textures began to appear. There was a gap in it and the boat headed for that.

A moment later, with the engines still rumbling, Tynan dropped over the side. The warm water was nearly chest deep. He waded toward the shore but stopped before climbing up onto the bank. In the dark, he was sure to leave footprints and gouges that would tell anyone who looked that someone had climbed out of the river. As the boat's engines began to roar and the boat backed away, Tynan diverted to the right toward a thick branch that dipped into the water. He used it to hoist himself from the water, being careful with his feet. Once on solid ground, he eased to the left and waited for his men.

One by one they joined him, each of them avoiding the open area where the mud would show their prints. When they were all on shore, formed in a rough defensive circle, Tynan made a quick head count. They were all assembled and no one had lost any equipment. He then took a compass reading, assuming for the moment that the PBR crew had put them ashore right where they were supposed to be or at least close enough that it wouldn't make a great deal of difference.

Jones moved out on the point, taking it slow and easy. James and Callahan became the flankers and Tynan figured he would bring up the rear. That left Mathis and Webb in the center. Each of the men had one of the small radios with instructions to break squelch twice if they saw the enemy, wait and then break squelch once for each enemy soldier. Three in quick succession meant that it was all clear and one long one was a call for help. They wouldn't speak unless something weird happened. That way it would be impossible for the enemy to triangulate on them or to intercept their messages.

For the first ten or twelve feet, the jungle was fairly thin, but then they got into it—a thick, dense growth that blotted out the sky above and made it impossible to see more than a few feet. The patrol drew in so that the men could see one another in the blackness. They moved around the bushes and slipped under the vines. They could have chopped their way through, but that would have left signs for the enemy to read and betrayed their presence. Tynan wanted them to move through the jungle with as little sign of their passing as possible. It slowed them, but didn't give them away.

With the sun gone, the humidity that had wrapped them as they had moved upriver seemed to evaporate. The sweat dried, leaving them fairly cool. That seemed to inspire them. Jones picked up the pace, using a walking stick to test the ground in front of him.

Someone had taken pains to teach Webb how to travel in the thick vegetation of a jungle, for even with the new guy in the center of the patrol, Tynan could hear only an occasional rustling of brush. Given the circumstances, there wasn't a thing he could do about it except live with it. He hoped that any enemy soldiers who might hear it would think that it was a monkey or the wind.

After nearly two hours, they stopped, forming a loose circle with every other man on alert. Tynan slipped into the center of the circle and used his poncho liner to cover himself. When he was sure that he had the edges on the ground all around him, he turned on a small penlight and studied the map. With the terrain being almost flat, it was hard to tell whether they were climbing into the interior or descending toward the coast. There were no outstanding terrain features that he could spot at night to shoot a compass course. All he had to go on was the position where the boat had left them and the compass headings they had used. He had to guess at the distance they had come. If everything had been done right and he guessed right on the distance, he knew exactly where they were. If it hadn't been, then they were lost. He wouldn't be able to tell for sure until morning.

That meant that he should stay where he was until he could check the location. If there was some miscalculation, but they kept moving, that would make the mistake worse. If they stayed put, it would be easy to correct it in the morning.

"Skipper?"

Tynan started at the quiet voice near his head. He knew that he was spending too much time under the poncho. He touched his sweat-damp face with the sleeve of his fatigues. He snapped off the light, waited for a moment as his eyes readjusted, and then whipped off the poncho liner. Cool air surrounded him immediately and he gulped in lungfuls.

"Skipper?"

Tynan leaned close and recognized Jones. "Camp here for tonight. We'll get a good sighting in the morning and plan from there."

"Aye, aye."

"Two-hour watches with Webb exempted. I want him in the center of the circle."

Jones didn't say anything, just moved off to inform the others. With him gone, Tynan moved back so that he could take his place in the defensive circle. As he lay down on his belly, staring out into the jungle, he knew that he wouldn't sleep now. The Dexedrine hadn't had the chance to wear off. He shouldn't have taken it on the boat. He should have waited until he'd had the chance to check out the situation. Now it would be another twenty-four hours before he got any sleep.

After the arrangements were made and the men were tied together by strings on their little fingers, Tynan tried to relax. He studied the ground around him, memorizing the bushes and the trees, watching for the enemy. He listened to the sounds of the jungle: the scratching as insects, some of them six inches long, ran across the rotting vegetation; the quiet scrambling in the trees as animals moved there; a low chatter of night birds; and as the sun started to rise, the noise of the monkeys as they came awake screaming at each other.

Without being told, each of the men got ready to move. They ate a quick, quiet breakfast from the rations they carried. Instead of burying the remains as usual, they put the garbage into their packs; the last thing they wanted was to leave any sign for the enemy, even if that sign was the remains of a C-ration breakfast.

After Tynan satisfied himself that they were where they were supposed to be, Callahan took point. Jones was detailed to remain behind and wipe out any sign that they had been there. He had ten minutes to do it and then would become the rear guard.

At first it was cool in the jungle. But as the sun climbed higher the heat began to bake the tops of the canopy. It filtered down, warming them, much like a steam bath. The moisture began to steam from the jungle floor until it seemed that each of the men was wrapped in a hot, wet blanket.

Tynan wanted to make up for the time lost the night before, but by midday it was obvious that the men wouldn't hold up. It was too hot, and trying to work their way through the thick undergrowth without chopping it was taking a heavy toll. The intense humidity was sapping their strength. The men were beginning to drag, they were getting sloppy and making noise. He called a halt.

Once again they fanned out in a loose circle with Webb protected in the center of it. Half of them were on alert while the other half rested or ate or drank water. Tynan told them not to move unless they had to once they had gotten themselves situated deep in the bush. They were away from the trail, so it was unlikely that anyone would stumble over them.

Late in the afternoon, Tynan told them to get ready to move out. They policed the area as best they could, picking up everything that belonged to them. He gave Callahan point again and gave him a compass course to follow. Then, with the sun still high in the sky, they began to move through the glowing green of the jungle.

They hadn't traveled far when Tynan heard the squelch on his radio snap twice. He dropped to one knee as did

the men around him. He snapped off the safety of his
CAR-15. Moments later there were twelve more clicks
telling him that a dozen of the enemy were moving
through the area.

Without a word, Tynan went to his belly, sliding to the
rear. He kept moving until he was next to a tall teak tree.
He reached out and touched the smooth bark. By lifting
his head slightly, he could see Webb and Jones. Both
seemed to freeze the moment the radio told them the enemy was near.

Tynan listened but could hear nothing other than the
constant chirp of the birds and the calls of the monkeys.
Slowly, he slid his hand along the stock of his weapon
until he touched the selector switch, moving it from single shot to auto. He kept his finger on the trigger and
watched for movement in the jungle around him.

The minutes crawled and still he heard nothing. There
was no sign of the enemy patrol and there was no shooting from Callahan. He hadn't asked for help, so Tynan
was sure that he was still alive and safe. Still, he wanted
to go check. He wanted to do something to find out what
was happening. The sitting around waiting was beginning
to get to him.

He had about convinced himself that it was time to
move when he had another thought: patience was the
thing that was hardest to teach Americans. They became
impatient easily, moving to investigate when, if they
would remain silent and quiet, nothing would happen. It
was the lesson that Tynan had been taught by the SAS in
England as he sat facing the blank face of the barn. Don't
be tempted into premature action, because that will get
you killed as quickly as anything.

So rather than move, Tynan put his trust in Callahan.
If his situation had somehow been compromised, Tynan

was sure he would have let them know. One round fired would have done it, and Tynan couldn't believe that the NVA or V.C. could take Callahan without the SEAL having a chance to warn his friends.

The solution, then, was to lay still, listen, and wait. Think of something else. Watch the ground around him and search for the enemy, but don't move.

The gnats came as the sun dropped closer to the horizon. The slanting rays penetrated the jungle in ways that those from overhead could not and that seemed to stir the gnats. They flickered on the edge of his vision, flitting in and out, darting at his eyes. Tynan wanted to swat at them but knew better than to make such a movement. He had to ignore them.

And then, finally, came the three quick breaks in the squelch that told him the enemy had moved off. Slowly, Tynan got to his feet. His muscles were stiff from the inactivity. He flexed them, getting the blood to circulate. He then moved forward along the line of march until he found Callahan crouched near a huge flowering bush.

"Dozen of them, Skipper. NVA, not V.C. They stopped for a break about ten yards from here. I thought they were setting up camp for the night."

"You sure they were NVA?"

"No question about it. Wore khaki, not black pajamas. Good discipline too."

Tynan nodded and whispered back, "You sure on the head count?"

"Yes, sir. Counted twelve coming in and twelve going out. Waited until they were out of sight and then gave them another fifteen minutes."

"Good. I'll put Mathis on point now that we've all had an extra rest. We're going to have to hump it now if we expect to get to that camp anytime soon."

When the rest of the patrol caught up, Tynan rotated the point men, putting Mathis out in front. They followed a moment later, staying as far apart as possible.

As the sun disappeared, they slowed until their pace was little better than a crawl, but they continued moving quietly through the darkened jungle, listening to the sounds made by the night creatures and listening to the sounds of the war drifting on the light breeze. Tynan had them stop every hour for a ten-minute rest because he felt they were getting close.

Finally at four he caught up to Mathis, who was lying next to a bush. Tynan crouched near him and put his lips next to Mathis's ear. "What's the problem?"

"No problem, Skipper. We've arrived."

Tynan turned and looked. Over the top of the grass and between the trunks of the trees he could see a light gray area. The longer he stared, the more he could see: hootches that weren't much more than bamboo poles with palm leaves for walls and roofs; and near the center a cage or two, and a man standing with his back to them. There was a hint of smoke in the air and a strange noise that Tynan identified as one of the enemy soldiers in the camp pissing in the jungle.

"Now what?" Mathis asked.

"Now we fall back, regroup, and look for a place from which to spy on the camp. That'll give us the information so that we can hit it tomorrow after dusk."

"You sure?"

Tynan nodded, and then realized that Mathis wouldn't be able to see the movement in the dark. "Positive. Tomorrow by this time we should be heading back to the river for pickup."

"I hope you're right."

"Don't worry. I am."

4

For several minutes Tynan watched the enemy camp. He searched for movement but saw little. Slowly he pulled the binoculars from his pack and used them. They brought the camp closer and made it seem brighter, enhancing the little available light. There were now three hootches visible. Two of them were little more than bamboo platforms with roofs of palm leaves. The sides were open and the floor was two or three feet off the ground. There were dark lumps on them that could have been supplies—or it could be sleeping men. The last, set back farther, was more substantial. It had mud sides and a thatch roof. A dim light flickered in the window there and Tynan suspected that the V.C. officers would be in there. It made it a target for the attack.

After watching for a while, Tynan spotted a guard standing next to a tree. He was little more than a black smudge hidden among the tangle of branches and vines that hung down along the trunk of the tree. He'd have never seen him if the man hadn't suddenly doubled over coughing. The sound and the movement drew Tynan's attention.

But that was all he could see. The canopy over the camp cut out most of the starlight and the moonlight, so that other than the single light from the hootch window, there was no illumination. Tynan put his binoculars away and eased to the rear. When he was far enough from the enemy that he wouldn't be seen, he got to his hands and knees and finally to his feet. When he reached the rest of the patrol, he crouched near them to brief them.

"Jones," he whispered, "I want you and Callahan to circle to the north and find a place to watch the camp. Note movements of their troops and try to get an accurate head count. Lay low through the day and return here in twenty-four hours so we can compare notes."

Jones didn't speak, simply nodded his understanding, touched Callahan on the shoulder, and disappeared into the bush. Tynan hadn't had to tell him to maintain radio silence unless he got into trouble. He hadn't had to mention a dozen things because he knew that Jones knew them already. Jones would watch the camp, collect his data, and remain out of sight.

"Mathis, I want you to remain here with James and Webb. Either you or James kept watch, and keep Webb hidden for now. If, after watching the camp, you think that he can get into a position to take a few pictures without tipping our hand, try to get that done. In twenty-four hours be back at this location. I'll be on the south side doing the same thing as everyone else."

"Skipper," said Mathis, "I can go with you and let James and Webb handle things here."

"No. I want the two of you to keep an eye on Webb and see that he gets his pictures."

Without waiting for a response, Tynan slipped away. He moved cautiously, stepping around the obstacles or sliding under them. He was careful where he put his feet but the jungle was damp, it having rained only a couple of days earlier. There hadn't been a chance for it to dry out with the humidity hovering near 100 percent.

He crossed a trail that looked as if it had seen heavy use recently. He hesitated there, watched and listened, and then crossed it quickly. He dropped into the vegetation on the other side and listened again. When it was evident that no one was following him or using the trail or searching for him, he continued on.

He circled around the camp and tried to approach from the south but the jungle there seemed to have formed an impenetrable wall. It started at the ground and ended two hundred feet in the air. He worked his way along it slowly, looking for a break.

After searching for nearly an hour, he found the perfect place. He crawled through the wall of the jungle and found that he was up above the camp, looking down from a slight ridge. The cover was thick and by creeping through it, he left no easily visible sign. He settled in, shedding his pack. He took one of his canteens and set it near the pack. He arranged everything the way he wanted it and then stopped moving. He would hardly breathe for the next ten or twelve hours.

He wanted to sleep, but without a partner he didn't dare. Besides, the Dexedrine was still in his system. Under its influence he could hear the quietest of sounds. Tiny claws of small animals as they ran through the jungle. A voice from the camp, singing softly. Night birds overhead. The distant pop of a helicopter's rotor. Through the ground he felt the vibrations of a B-52 strike so far away that he couldn't hear it.

Again he used his binoculars. From the new angle, he could see a couple more hootches constructed along the lines of the first few he had seen. In the center were several cages, but there was no movement in them. Tynan watched them for a long time, but his angle was wrong so he couldn't tell if they were empty or not. To one side, near the trunk of a giant tree, was a small structure. There were no windows in it, only a closed door. During the day it had to be miserable inside.

He wished he could get a count of the number of guards, but no one was moving around in the night. He wanted to get a map of their locations too. He wondered if the enemy patrol they had run into had come from this camp, or if it had originated somewhere else. If it had originated here, that would mean that there were more than just guards in the camp, which would mean that he was badly outnumbered.

Then he decided not to worry about it. The morning would provide the answers. He would be able to see most of the guards then and would get a glance at the prisoners. All he had to do was lie low and let the enemy give himself away. Again, it was patience that was the answer.

He put his binoculars down and waited for morning, listening to the ebb and flow of the jungle. From somewhere distant came the cry of a cat. Then, for some reason Tynan remembered the spiders they had found one day. Huge things nearly a foot across that had hidden in the dark crevasses and that had come swarming out as the smoke from the grenade they had thrown blew into the rocky face of a cliff. The men—SEALS who had been in some of the worst situations imaginable—had nearly panicked at the sight. One of them had opened fire, emptying a whole clip into the creatures. But the spiders had fled, almost as if the sunlight hurt them, disappearing into cracks in the rock face.

Now the thought of those spiders came back. He could feel his skin crawl as he was sure that a dozen of them were stalking him. His back itched and he thought he could feel something on his legs. He ignored it.

The night passed slowly. There was a moment of false dawn and then the trees above him exploded into noise. Monkeys began swinging through the trees, screaming at each other. They rattled the branches, hung under them, and chattered at the tops of their lungs. The racket drowned out everything else. They kept at it for nearly twenty minutes as the jungle brightened around him.

And then, as though someone had flipped a switch, the jungle was quiet. The monkeys stopped screaming. They swung through the treetops shaking the branches, occasionally calling to one another, but it wasn't the constant, loud noise that it had been. But as they quieted, the birds started. A constant chirping and calling that became the background noise of the jungle.

The camp came awake with the rising of the sun and the screaming of the monkeys. There was no way that the men in it could sleep through the racket. At first there were vague shapes moving among the hootches, but as it got lighter, the shapes changed into humans. One man left a platformed hootch that had been hidden in the darkness of the night. Dropping to the ground, he scurried to a small mud hootch, which he disappeared into. Then he came back out and lit a fire. The smoke was dissipated by a series of barriers above it so that nothing climbed into the canopy.

Other men began moving. Guards left their posts on the perimeter of the camp, moving toward the hootch where the man had begun cooking breakfast. They stacked their weapons, a mixture of guns manufactured by the Soviet Union and Red China, and captured from the South Vietnamese. There were AK-47s, SKSs, M1s and M1 carbines, and even two M16s.

As it got brighter, Tynan spotted men locked in the cages. He put the binoculars on them. Each was shackled, the leg irons leading from raw, bleeding ankles to posts driven into the ground. Each wore rags that had been uniforms and all of the men he could see were Vietnamese. They were tired-looking, skinny men, who moved slowly, as if they were very old. They were sick and mistreated.

One of the guards carried a bucket toward the cages and set it down on the outside so that the men in the cage couldn't reach it. He squatted there, lifting some of the stuff in the bucket up with a spoon so that the men in the cages could see it. Then, laughing, he dropped the spoon back into the bucket and walked away.

Another guard took a similar bucket to the closed hootch near the tree. He opened the door, set it inside, and then left. Tynan knew that the Americans—if they were in the camp—would be held in that hootch. No opportunity for escape and no opportunity to communicate with the South Vietnamese prisoners, no opportunity to do anything. The last thing the V.C. or NVA would want would be for the Americans to escape.

Tynan turned his attention back to the men held in the cages. Another of the guards walked over to the bucket, kicked the side of it, and then peered down into it. Finally he moved it close enough to the cage for the Vietnamese to get to it.

Throughout the morning Tynan watched the routine of the camp. Guards circulating, some of them armed with rifles, others carrying large sticks. They herded the Vietnamese out of the cages and made them perform a variety of tasks such as cleaning out the cooking shed and cleaning the hootches used by the V.C. and NVA.

An armed guard was placed on the closed hootch, but no one ever appeared at the doorway, so Tynan couldn't confirm the presence of the Americans. He had to go on the documents they had found claiming Americans were being held, since he wasn't getting any visual confirmation of it.

At noon there was another meal served to the guards and the staff of the tiny camp, but the Vietnamese prisoners, and the men in the hootch were not fed. Instead, the Vietnamese stood in a short line near their captors watching them dine on rice, fish, and stolen C-rations.

After that meal was finished, the prisoners were moved to the edge of the camp. They sat in rows, their backs straight, and waited until an officer came from his hootch at the far side of the camp. He walked toward them slowly, sipping from a glass holding a brown beverage that could have been iced tea or a Coke. As he reached them, he drained the last of the liquid and handed the empty glass to one of the guards. He smacked his lips noisily and then began a speech in rapid Vietnamese. Tynan was conversant in Vietnamese, but only caught a few words; nonetheless, he was sure it was some kind of an indoctrination course.

When he tired of watching the man strutting in front of the prisoners slapping his left hand with a stick held in the right, Tynan turned his attention to the closed hootch. The guards rotated frequently, but no one ever appeared at the door. Hell, no one ever entered it, except that one man earlier in the day. The enemy watched it closely, but gave no clue as to what it was. If it hadn't been for the bucket taken in earlier, Tynan would have believed that it was some kind of weapons locker. But a weapons locker would have no use for a bucket of food—if it *was* food in the bucket.

As the afternoon burned on, Tynan ate some of his C-rations and drank some of his water. The treat of the day was the peaches. He ate them slowly and drank the juice. He moved slowly, cautiously, not wanting to give the enemy anything to spot. He kept his eyes moving, watching the guards. He tried to figure out their routine. They didn't seem inclined to form patrols or even sweep the perimeter. They stayed in the background while the officer continued his class, lecturing the prisoners in a voice that seemed excessively loud for a hideout in the jungle.

The thing that struck Tynan was that he had seen no patrols either leave or return to the camp. That meant that the duty had fallen to another group who had their own compound somewhere else. They could be a click away, or two or ten, or they could be within a hundred meters—although, if they were that close, Tynan was sure that one of his men would have spotted them. It meant that there could be a large enemy force in easy striking distance, so he would have to plan his raid carefully.

In the late afternoon, the prisoners were returned to their cages. One man moved among them, fastening the shackles to their ankles and testing the chains by trying to yank them free. When he finished, the cage doors were locked and the guards returned to their hootches.

Tynan watched as the men disappeared. He had tried to count the number of enemy soldiers in the camp. Even though some of them might have stayed out of sight all day, for whatever reason, and he might have counted some men more than once, he was still fairly sure that there were fewer than thirty enemy soldiers in the camp. Thirty men to guard the twelve South Vietnamese and the men being held in the solid hootch.

As the sun began to drop, the green glow going out of the camp, the guards appeared. They moved out into the jungle, taking positions close to where they had been the night before. Apparently Charlie didn't expect the Americans to sneak in to watch them. They were getting sloppy.

Once he saw that, Tynan started to retreat. He gathered his gear quietly, moving with the slowest of motions, his eyes on the enemy camp. He didn't bother with carrying his empty C-ration cans. Before anyone found them, he was sure that he would be out of the area.

Whenever anyone in the camp glanced in his direction, he froze. But that didn't happen often. When he was ready, he slipped from hiding. He crawled backwards, keeping watch on the enemy camp. As the last of the light disappeared, he got to his feet. For a moment he stood still, letting the blood circulate so that feeling returned to his limbs. He had been lying quietly for so long that it took several minutes.

Tynan then moved to the rear. He walked carefully, slowly, measuring each step before he took it, careful not to make noise. Overhead, in the interlocking branches of the canopy, he could hear a breeze rattling and the buzz and singing of the night insects.

Tynan moved in on his men quietly. As he saw the first dark shape, he realized that the man had been watching him. Tynan crouched, one knee on the ground. For a moment he stared at the man, and then saw the others come in.

"Okay," he said, "I think we've got enough to move in."

He waited until they all nodded their agreement. In the darkness of the jungle, it was hard to see them, especially with their faces smeared with camouflage paint. But their noses were only inches apart so that Tynan's voice was quiet and impossible to hear more than two feet away.

He then outlined his plan. Stealth was the key. If they could slip in, taking out only a few of the guards, and then open the sealed hootch before vanishing into the night, they might get away with it. A sneak-and-peek operation. If they had to shoot, it would mean that they would have to kill nearly everyone in the camp and there was still that patrol wandering around behind them—not to mention the possibility of another camp somewhere close.

They would run it just like the V.C. would. Go in on one side, using their knives to kill the men in the way. If they could get to the Vietnamese, they should be rescued, too, but that would be a target of opportunity. He also wanted one or two men to stay behind and set up the claymores. If, as the men retreated, they were being followed, the claymores would slow down the pursuit. If not, they could pick them up. It was a very simple plan that relied on stealth and luck.

After he had finished giving the assignments—who would stay back to cover, who would set the claymores to cover the retreat, and who would make the recon into the camp—he asked for questions. He looked from face to face, waiting, giving each man a chance to ask something or to criticize.

"Nothing?"

Jones said, "We don't shoot?"

"Not unless you have to. At that point, we rush the sealed the hootch, kick open the door, and get the men out. Once we secure that, we all get the hell out. If we have to, we'll escape and evade to the north with anyone we get out of there. We rendezvous at the river if we get separated."

"What time do we go?" asked Callahan.

Tynan glanced at his wrist but didn't check the time. It was a reflex action. "I think we should rest for a couple hours and go in about two in the morning. That's when everything should be at a low ebb. We should be out within thirty minutes. We'll get a good jump on them and then hole up until dawn."

Tynan then looked from face to face. He could see the eyes and little else. He knew that they were breathing but couldn't hear a sound from it. He waited for them to speak again or ask another question, but no one did. Finally he nodded and said, "Let's spread out and get some rest. We go in just over three hours."

5

Tynan jerked awake and realized that it had to be about time to begin. He lay quietly, listening to the jungle around him, making sure that there hadn't been some kind of change that had awakened him. A sudden silence where they had been the chirping and buzzing of insects, or a snapping of a twig where there shouldn't have been one.

When he was convinced that he had awakened because it was almost time for the attack, he shifted around to survey the vegetation in front of him, but there was no indication that the enemy was alerted. Slowly he moved his hand until he pulled back the camouflage band on his watch. The dimly glowing numbers told him it was now one-thirty.

Tynan rolled to his back and sat up. He reached for his canteen and took a deep drink that tasted of warm plastic and the halazone tablets used to purify the water. It was a bad taste that did little to clean his mouth. He sloshed the water around his mouth but didn't spit it out. When he had finished, he capped the canteen and got to his feet. He moved along the line until he came to Callahan, who was still watching the enemy camp.

"What's going on?"

"They changed the guard about ten minutes ago. They've only got five guys out now. They don't seem to be taking this guard stuff seriously."

"You have all the guards spotted?"

"Of course."

"Show me."

Callahan described the positions that each of the guards had taken. The process was slow because neither man wanted to point and they had to be very quiet. Tynan searched the jungle and brush until he had each of them spotted. The only reason he succeeded was because the enemy didn't try to hide. They moved around, scratched, swatted at insects, and one of them was even smoking. The glowing tip of his cigarette marked his position like a beacon at an airport.

As Callahan finished pointing out the guards, the rest of the team appeared. Tynan checked the time and then said, "We're going to delay by fifteen minutes. Since there are five guards and five of us, we'll take them all out. All five of them at the same time."

Then, one by one, he assigned the targets. As each man received his assignment, he moved off until all of them were moving through the jungle with the exception of Webb. It was his job to hang back and guard the packs. If something happened to the patrol, he was to use a grenade to destroy the equipment and then was to get out. His pictures would have to be enough.

When each of the men had moved off, Tynan crept into the jungle. He moved through the loose perimeter, by-passing the guards there. Tynan figured he would take the guard closest to the sealed hootch.

He circled to the east and then turned north. He moved quietly, carefully setting his feet on the ground, heel first, and rotating the foot. It made walking difficult, a strain on the lower leg, but it kept him from making noise. He ducked under a couple of thick branches and slipped around the large trunk of a tree. He stopped twice and listened, but the sounds of the jungle hadn't changed.

There was no indication that the enemy guards even suspected that an American patrol was close to them.

He kept moving slowly, rhythmically. As he approached the edge of the jungle that marked the inner perimeter of the camp, he got to his hands and knees and continued to crawl. Finally he stopped and went down to his belly. He could feel the moisture of the jungle seeping through his uniform—Cold, clammy water squeezed up from the rotting leaves and dying plants. He ignored the feeling, his eyes on the man whose head kept dropping to his chest fifty meters in front of him. Then forty and thirty. His victim was trying to stay awake on the late-night guard detail, and having little luck.

Tynan slung his weapon then, making sure that he was tightly fastened down. The last thing he needed was for it to snag on something or rattle against his equipment. He reached up and grabbed the knife that had been taped to the left side of his harness and drew it out. The combat knife had a blade with a flat black finish so that it couldn't reflect light. It was razor sharp.

Again, Tynan checked the time. He measured the distance between him and the guard and began to work his way forward. He was approaching the enemy from the left side. As he neared, the man jerked awake and looked around wildly. Tynan froze, trying to become a bush, hoping that he could blend into the jungle around him. Hoping that the Vietcong soldier wouldn't notice the black shape that had moved nearer to him. He held his breath and lowered his eyes, afraid that he would communicate with the man through ESP. After the soldier settled down and his head began nodding again, Tynan started moving.

He halted only a couple of feet behind the enemy soldier, slowly getting to his hands and knees. He shifted his feet so that they were under him. He waited a moment, watching the Vietcong. There was a sudden, quiet commotion to the right. The man's head snapped up and he grabbed at his rifle, pointing it at the sound and half turning toward it. As he did, Tynan leaped. In one fluid motion, he kicked the rifle from the enemy's hand, reached around him, and grabbed his face. Clamping a hand over the soldier's nose and mouth, he slashed at the man's throat, feeling the knife bite the flesh. There was a momentary resistance and then the blade pulled free. Tynan felt the blood splash and smelled its faint copper odor.

The man slumped downward, a groan in his throat. Tynan struck a second time, forcing the blade up under the rib cage to puncture the lungs and heart. The Vietcong drummed one foot on the ground as Tynan dragged him to the rear. He teeth clenched, pinching the flesh of Tynan's hand. Then all the enemy's muscles relaxed completely as he died. There was the overpowering odor of bowel.

Tynan rolled the man into the bush. He crouched there, his nerves taunt, his senses singing. Everything around him seemed to brighten. He could hear the tiniest of noises. He could smell the faintest odors. He turned toward the front of the camp and saw one of his men moving toward the cages, a black shape bent nearly double, running silently.

Tynan wiped the blade of his knife on the dead man's shirt and then slipped it into his scabbard. He picked up the enemy's weapon and broke it open, taking out the bolt, which he dropped into his pocket, and leaving the AK on the ground.

As he moved toward the sealed hootch, he unslung his own weapon. His fingers felt the side of it and he pushed the selector switch from safe to full auto. Still there was no indication that the Vietcong were aware that they were being attacked. Tynan moved through the grass and bush that separated him from the sealed hootch.

Again he stopped short and listened. There was a chill on the night and a breeze in the treetops above him. He could smell dirt and sweat and shit. He crouched next to a small bush and surveyed the ground around him: nothing of interest. Short grass, some of it flattened by the feet of the guards and the prisoners as they walked around the camp. Saplings that grew throughout the area, and the trunks of huge trees.

Tynan started to work his way forward when he sensed something near him. He froze and turned his head slowly. Out of the gloom came another enemy soldier. His bare skin was reflecting the little light that seeped into the area. He held one hand on his stomach and was digging at his crotch with the other, chuckling deep in his throat.

Without waiting to see if the man had seen him or had merely stepped out for a piss, Tynan struck again. He grabbed the V.C. by the throat, squeezing the air from it. His knee came up and smashed the enemy in the groin. There was a startled gasp as the V.C.'s knees buckled, and as the man slipped to the ground, Tynan used his hand to smash his throat. The enemy dropped to his back, his feet pounding on the soft earth. Tynan then used the butt of his CAR-15 to smash the man's nose, driving bits of bone into the brain to kill him quickly.

Crouched over the body, he listened to the jungle around him: nothing. Then from somewhere to his right, near the shed that was the cookhouse, there was a burst from an M16, a quick ripping as someone fired. From the sound, Tynan was sure it was one of his men.

Callahan had worked his way through the jungle until he was close to the perimeter of the tiny camp. For a moment he crouched there, his face pressed close to the ground. He didn't want to think about the coming few minutes. If he thought about it, he would get nervous and that might cause him to make mistakes. All he wanted was to concentrate on a cold beer served by a lovely lady. A loving lady, he amended.

He was aware of the sweat trickling down his sides and back—sweat that was not born of heat and humidity, but from the fear that was knotting his stomach. He touched his lips with his wrist and tried to imagine how the beer would taste, and what the girl would look like. She would have short, blond hair, he decided. Short and blond so that she wouldn't look anything like a Vietnamese.

Finally he got to his feet, his fingertips on the ground for balance as he hunched over and searched the dark jungle for his target. He spotted the dark shape as the man, shifting his weight, transferred his weapon from one hand to the other.

Callahan slung his weapon, drawing his knife. He wanted to clench it in his teeth as the pirates in the movies always did, but he didn't want to cut the hell out of his mouth. Instead, he held on to the hilt, his thumb near the top of the blade. Blinking the sweat from his eyes, he began to creep forward, watching his target carefully.

The Vietcong suspected nothing. He stood with his back to Callahan, staring into the treetops as if he could see something fascinating there. Maybe he was looking for monkeys. Maybe he was daydreaming. Callahan couldn't believe his luck. It was as if the enemy were asking to have his throat cut.

When he was only a few feet from the man, Callahan rose to his full height and stepped forward, his left foot out in front of him. With his left hand, he seized the man, clamping over his nose and mouth. As the enemy went down, he tossed his rifle to his side, where it fell to the ground with a thud. He reached up then, one hand clawing at the air and the other seizing Callahan's arm, trying to jerk it off his mouth. But it was already too late. Callahan was dragging him to the rear, the man's back on the fulcrum of his knee. At the same time, he was lifting the chin and cutting the throat. The man's blood was pounding from his body as his heart hammered in fear.

A spurt of blood splashed upward. Callahan heard it on the leaves of the plants and on the grass, sounding like rain in the evening. He felt the warmness as it washed over his hand and smelled it as it soaked his uniform.

As the man died, bent back over Callahan's knee, his throat a bloody, gaping wound, Callahan dropped the body to the ground. He then froze, listening, but could only hear his own blood pounding in his ears. His hand was shaking as he wiped the blade on the dead man's clothes.

He moved then, stepping to the cover of a small bush. He slipped his knife into its scabbard and unslung his weapon. Around him, he knew the other guards were dying, but he heard and saw nothing of that. The remainder of the SEALS were executing their mission perfectly. Callahan wished he had done as well. The death of the guard had been sloppy. He had lived too long after Callahan attacked.

Callahan stood and eased to the right. He turned and collided with another man. As both of them fell, Callahan knew that it was another Vietnamese. He saw the man sit up and reach for a weapon. Not hesitating, Callahan pulled the trigger of his M16. He fired five shots quickly, from the hip. In the muzzle flashes that lit the man's face like the strobe of a camera, Callahan could see the surprise and fear. The enemy dropped to the ground without a sound.

* * *

James was the closest to his position, so he had been detailed to lay the claymores to cover the retreat. He set them up so that the enemy, if he was following, would walk into the mechanical ambush. He was at the edge of the light jungle where Charlie had built his camp. He aimed the claymores into it and strung out the firing cables, draping them over a low-hanging branch where he could find them again easily. Then, in case he couldn't get back to them, he wired a couple of them as booby traps. Charlie, blundering down the trail, would set off one or two of the claymores.

When he finished rigging that, he moved forward, crawling low until he could see the enemy soldier in front of him. He stopped, watched the man, and realized he was asleep. There was no question about it. As he eased his way closer, he could hear the man snoring.

James stopped, lying in the grass near a bush, and studied the enemy camp. Although he knew there were four other guards and four other SEALS stalking them, he could see no signs of them.

He set his weapon on the ground, the operating rod up, out of the dirt. He rolled to his left and drew his knife. This was going to be so simple that it was almost ridiculous. The man would never know what hit him.

Pulling off the camouflage band, he checked his watch. When it was time, he got to his feet. In a low crouch, he moved in on the sleeping man and stopped right behind him. The man was sleeping with his chin on his chest: it made cutting his throat difficult.

He was just about to put his knife back in the scabbard and try to snap the V.C.'s neck when the man started. His snore was more of a snort and his head snapped up. He glanced around and then settled back.

That was James's signal. The SEAL stepped across the last few feet of open ground. He snagged the man under the chin, almost missing his grip, pulled the head up and back, and slashed with the knife. Since his hand cupped the chin, rather than covering the mouth, James cut deep to sever the vocal cords, so that the man couldn't cry out.

In his surprise, the man dropped his rifle. He grabbed at James, digging his fingers into the SEAL's arm, but it was too late. James felt him go rigid and then limp. When the man was dead, James stretched him out on the ground, picked up the rifle, and retreated into the jungle.

When he found the firing controls for the claymores, he stopped. He found a good place to watch the camp and settled in. He grinned, thinking they had it made. No one would know they were there, or had been there, until the dead guards were found in the morning. A perfect terror raid.

And then came the shots from the camp and James knew that the game was up.

Jones, on the south side of the camp, had reached his man but not yet attacked. The soldier had suddenly decided that he was standing too still and had begun to move in a small circle, perhaps trying to stay awake. Jones had to wait until the man's back was turned, then move closer, trying to anticipate the next change in direction. He would freeze, afraid to breathe until the Vietcong turned again.

Just as he reached him, the shots sounded. The enemy froze, facing the sound. There was a shout and the Vietcong worked the bolt of his weapon. As he did, Jones attacked. From the rear, Jones cupped the man's chin, lifting it as he drew his knife across the soft flesh. He didn't worry about the textbook now, because somebody was shooting. When the man sagged slightly, Jones jammed the knife into his back, aiming it upward, toward the heart and lungs. The enemy dropped to his knees and fell forward, ripping the knife from Jones's hand. He never made a sound.

But now there was shouting all over the camp. A light flashed and then went out. There was a burst from an AK-47, but the green tracers seemed to be aimed into the treetops, not at any target on the ground. There were single shots and then another burst.

As shooting broke out around the camp, all from AKs, Jones hit the ground, crawling to the left toward a huge bush. He grabbed a grenade and yanked the pin free, but didn't throw it, because he wasn't sure where the rest of the team members were. Besides, he didn't have a target. He didn't want to use his rifle if he could help it. The muzzle flash would tell the Vietcong where he was.

He began to work his way into the center of the camp, watching the hootches where the guards slept. He saw one man crouched in the doorway, an AK in his hand, but the man wasn't shooting. Jones wished he had a silenced weapon so he could kill the man quietly. Instead, he got to his knees and tossed the grenade as if it were a baseball, aiming it at the man's head.

The man opened fire then, but wasn't shooting at Jones. He sprayed the jungle. The strobing of the muzzle flash made it look like the man was caught in an old movie. In the frames, Jones saw his grenade fly by the man's head. As it did, the enemy jerked around, searching.

The grenade exploded behind him, throwing him out the door. There was a rattling of shrapnel against the bamboo-and-palm-leaf walls of the hootch. The man landed with a thump and a grunt, but didn't move again. His weapon lay in front of his outstretched hand.

At the sound of the grenade, Tynan was on his feet, moving toward the sealed hootch. He was afraid the captives would be killed if the V.C. believed they were about to be overrun.

He dived to the ground and rolled over so that his side was against the wall of the structure. He put his ear against the crumbling mud, but heard nothing from the interior. He stood up, his back to the wall, and slipped to the right, his head turned so that he could see.

It was suddenly silent again. The shouting had stopped with the explosion of the grenade. Tynan halted at the end of the hootch. He dropped to one knee and peeked around the corner, but there was nothing to see now. No one moved. No one spoke. No one shot at the flickering shadows. The Vietcong were waiting for the attackers to show themselves, and Tynan's SEALS were smart enough not to let that happen.

Tynan pulled back and took a deep breath. With his thumb, he checked the selector switch on his CAR-15 a final time, making sure that it was set on full auto. Then he eased to the right so that he was next to the corner of the hootch. Again, he waited, but when no one in the camp moved, Tynan reached out. He touched the handle on the door and tried to open it.

Mathis was close to his man, but afraid to attack when the first burst of firing ripped through the camp. The Vietcong took two running steps forward, slid to a halt, and dropped to his knees. He raised his rifle, swinging it from side to side as if tracking birds flying overhead. He didn't fire it; he just kept aiming it.

Mathis took a single step and froze as the enemy soldier started to spin. Mathis fell forward, landing on his hands. His eyes were on the V.C. But then the grenade exploded in the barracks where the majority of the enemy soldiers were sleeping. The V.C. near Mathis mumbled something and stood up, aiming his weapon at the explosion.

As he did, Mathis leaped at him in one liquid motion, coming off the ground and drawing his knife at the same time. The man must have heard something because he turned. But Mathis was too close to him. He grabbed the rifle barrel in his left hand and struck with his right. The knife punched through the thin material of the black silk shirt. The enemy groaned in surprise and pain as his blood splashed. Mathis stepped back, drawing the knife free. He slashed at the V.C.'s throat, cutting it. Not exactly the way it was supposed to go, but it worked. The man released his grip on the rifle as he reached up to his bloody throat. There was a bubbling in his neck as his blood flowed down his chest.

Mathis kicked out then and the enemy collapsed to his side. As he tossed the rifle into the jungle and turned, Mathis saw the muzzle flashes from a weapon. He fell to the ground, rolling to his left so that he could get to his own gun. Another V.C. fired, the green tracers snapping over his head.

Mathis saw the man outlined by the muzzle flashes, and brought up his own weapon. He aimed at the middle of the muzzle flashes and opened up. His first shots were wide and drew some fire in return, so he rolled to the right and aimed again. He caught movement then and shot at it. There was a yell and a crash as someone fell to the ground.

Mathis was up then, running. He dodged first to the right, then to the left. Flames were beginning to show in the barracks. He saw a silhouette and fired at it. The figure doubled over, throwing his weapon out in front of him. Then he turned, as if to face Mathis, and fell from

the platform, landing flat on his back and not moving
again.

Mathis kept going. He leaped around one of the flimsy
hootches, a structure of palm leaves and bamboo, and
stopped. In front of him, Tynan was crouched, one hand
on the latch of the sealed hootch. He raised his rifle to
cover the lieutenant, and waited.

Tynan heard someone running toward him. He glanced
at the noise and recognized Mathis. He waited for the
other man to stop. Then he leaned forward, lifting the
latch. There was a quiet click and Tynan suddenly wondered why the hootch wasn't locked. If there were important prisoners in it, it should have been locked.

He hesitated, expecting a trap. He shifted his feet so
that he could spring in any direction and then took a deep
breath. Finally, he glanced at Mathis and saw that his
weapon was up. Tynan nodded, not sure that the other
man could see the gesture in the dark.

There were a dozen other things that he wanted to do,
but he realized that he was avoiding the door. His fingers
tightened around the pistol grip of his CAR-15. He inched
forward and pushed gently on the door. It started to swing
inward, silently and without any resistance.

He shoved it open violently and dodged back out of the
way. Mathis was on his feet then, moving toward it.
Tynan got to his feet, his back against the mud wall. He
watched Mathis come at him and as the other man jumped
to the left side of the door, Tynan leaped around the corner so that he was on the opposite side.

The interior of the structure was pitch black. Behind
them the flames in one of the barracks were beginning to
burn brighter, but that didn't help. Tynan tried to keep

from silhouetting himself. He dropped to one knee and hissed, "Anyone in there?"

He listened. Other than the sound of the sporadic firing and the detonation of a Chicom grenade, there was nothing. No indication that anyone was in the sealed hootch.

Tynan glanced at Mathis, who had moved up. He nodded and then leaped through the opening. He landed on a rough wood planking that smelled of sap. He rolled once and came up on his knee, his weapon pointed into the blackness. Although he listened intently, he was suddenly sure that there was no one in the hootch with him.

Mathis entered right behind him. He covered the other side and then asked, "What the fuck?"

"No one in here."

"But we saw—"

"There's no one in here," repeated Tynan. He got to his feet and took a position at the door. He could see the muzzle flashes of weapons of the V.C. and his SEALS as they fired at one another. There was a movement to the right. Tynan opened fire and cut down the enemy soldier.

"Let's get out of here," Tynan said.

"After you, Skipper."

Tynan hesitated in the doorway. The thing he wanted to do now was break contact. Now it was important that they get out of there before the enemy could organize any kind of counterattack or before reinforcements from the suspected bases could arrive.

Finally he said, "Let's get out of here."

6

Tynan waited for a moment, watching the shapes dance across the enemy compound. The flickering light from the fires started by the exploding grenades and the tracer rounds gave him enough light to see. The Vietnamese were small men who carried AK-47s, so that they had a distinct shape to them. There was no problem identifying targets. Tynan watched two of them run from the burning hootch, dodge around the cook's shed, and try to reach the safety of the jungle. They weren't interested in defending their camp, they just wanted to get the hell out of there. Before he could fire, one of his men opened up and both the Vietnamese died in a hail of bullets, some of them glowing ruby red.

He touched Mathis on the shoulder and pointed to the right where the jungle was the closest to them. "You go first. I'll cover."

Mathis nodded once but didn't move. Instead, he dropped the magazine from his weapon, reloading quickly with a fresh one. He scooped the partially used clip from the wooden floor and stuffed it into his pocket to use later. He glanced at Tynan and then out the door. When it seemed that everyone had his attention somewhere else, Mathis ran.

Tynan watched him go, covering him. As Mathis reached the edge of the jungle, one man loomed up behind him. A skinny man whose bare, sweaty skin reflected the firelight. The enemy soldier lifted his weapon to aim at Mathis. Tynan pointed his CAR-15 at the man and fired. The V.C. jerked with the impact of the rounds like a rag doll on a string. He fell forward facedown and didn't move.

Now Tynan was up and running. He glanced toward the center of the prison camp. One of his men was yanking on the lock that held a cage closed. Tynan changed direction, running to help him. As he reached the cages, another of the enemy appeared, seeming to grow out of the ground. Tynan slammed into him, knocking him from his feet. There was a grunt of pain and surprise. Tynan kicked upward, catching the man under the chin, snapping his head to the rear. He rolled to his back with a groan and didn't move again.

"Shoot it off," said Tynan.

Jones looked at him and put the barrel of his weapon next to the lock. He pulled the trigger once. The lock seemed to spin on the hasp and then flew upward.

"Got it," Jones said as he flipped open the hasp. He entered the cage and saw that the men were shackled to the poles driven into the ground. "Shit."

Tynan had dropped to one knee, watching the jungle and the camp to the south of the cage. Firing had broken out to the right, AK against M16. There were dull, quiet pops as the underpowered Chicom grenades detonated. Tynan wanted to lend support to his men fighting there, but wasn't sure of the targets. There was too little light and the men were too far away from him. Then there was a sustained burst that came from an M16. Ruby tracers danced through the jungle, bouncing into the sky. The AKs stopped shooting.

Glancing over his shoulder, Tynan hissed, "Hurry it up. We've got to get out of here."

Jones stood, his right side near the bamboo pole. He kicked out and there was a splintering of wood. He kicked again and then crouched, grabbing the chain. He flipped it over the broken stump of bamboo stake, freeing the men in that cage.

"Can you guys move?" he asked.

There was no response. He leaned close to them. Their eyes were wide with fright as if they didn't understand that it was a rescue. They cowered, trying to get away from the huge apparition with the dark green and black face. Jones leaned close and demanded, "English? Any of you speak English?" When that failed to produce a response, he tried French. One of the men answered him then.

"Get up," demanded Jones in French. "Get up and get out. Move it."

The Vietnamese suddenly seemed to understand what was happening. One by one they got to their feet, grabbing at the chain. As one, they moved from the cage and out into the compound. They hesitated there but then began to inch their way toward the protection of the jungle.

Tynan stood up and moved to the rear. Over his shoulder he could see the firefight on the western side of the camp. His men seemed to hold the perimeter while the Vietcong were trying to get into the jungle. They were funneling into the escape route that Callahan had discovered earlier and that James had mined before they began the raid.

"Any time," he said under his breath.

It was as if James had heard him. There was a series of explosions as the claymores exploded one by one, the flashing moving deeper into the jungle. There were shouts, screams of pain, shrieks from the dying as the steel balls burst outward in a killing arc. Even after the firing of the claymores, Tynan could hear the steel balls ripping through the vegetation, shredding it and the bodies of the enemy who had fled in that direction.

Suddenly it was quiet. No more shooting. No more running. Tynan stood flat-footed, breathing hard, and bent over. He gulped the hot, humid air, unable to get enough of it. The only sound was his blood hammering in his ears and his breath rasping in his throat. He turned as Jones approached.

"Skipper?"

"How many prisoners did you free?"

Jones shrugged and said, "A dozen."

"Let's get them out of here." He turned and led them toward the jungle in a low, fast formation. Once they left the compound, Tynan paused to look at the freed South Vietnamese silhouetted in the dim, flickering light from the burning hootches. Some of them were badly undernourished. Their legs were little thicker than bones; the skin on their faces was stretched tight, giving them a skeletal look: they couldn't travel far in the jungle.

"Jones, I'm heading for the rally point. You follow with the prisoners. When I get there, I'll get help to come back."

"Sure, Skipper."

Tynan didn't like the sound of Jones's voice, but there was nothing he could do about it now. He shrugged and pushed off into the dense vegetation. Now he wasn't worried about noise discipline. The enemy would know that they were in the area. The shooting had told them that. But with luck, the enemy was scattered and confused so the noise that Tynan made wouldn't be a problem. There were no Vietcong to act on the intelligence it provided.

He rushed forward, avoiding the big trees and the bushes, dodging right and left. In a few minutes he was close to the rally point. From the darkness he heard a challenge. One of his men making sure he was an American. Tynan answered it and then waited a moment. There was no reason to get shot by one of his men.

Finally he pushed his way through the last of the vegetation and came face-to-face with a grinning Mathis. "You get a muster for me?"

"Callahan and Webb are here. So's James after he punched off the claymores. We're missing Jones. No one seems to know where he is."

"You stay here with Webb," said Tynan. "Callahan, you're on me. James, you're in the rear about five, six meters back. Jones freed the South Vietnamese prisoners and we've got to help him bring them in."

Without a word, Callahan joined Tynan and together they moved back through the jungle. James hesitated a moment, letting them build a small lead and then followed. As they worked their way toward the points of light that were the dying embers from the fires, the insects began to sing again. There was a buzzing from the flies too. A night bird screamed somewhere behind them. Slowly the animals were beginning to return now that the firing had ended.

It took them ten minutes to get to Jones. Three of them got the South Vietnamese on their feet and moving while James stayed hidden and covered them. Jones had to carry one of the South Vietnamese and several had to be helped either by Tynan and Callahan or by their friends. They made noise moving through the jungle. Tynan knew that they were leaving a wide trail, if anyone felt inclined to follow—assuming that the Vietcong could get some kind of pursuit organized soon. There was nothing he could do about all the clues they were leaving.

Now they moved slowly. They couldn't afford to have one of the South Vietnamese injured in the dark. Callahan moved out on point, leaving Tynan to help the injured. Callahan kept the pace steady, but avoided the roughest of the terrain. James was back there somewhere covering the rear, but Tynan could hear no indication of him. That was as it should be.

After forty minutes, they made the rally point, this time unchallenged. Mathis knew that they were coming in and he had been watching them for a long time. Besides, he had heard them coming.

As soon as they had the former prisoners situated, Tynan got his men out as guards watching for a counterattack. He left Jones to take care of the South Vietnamese since he was the one who could speak French and who had some medical training. Mostly it was a matter of giving them water and finding them small amounts of food. The last thing they needed was for the South Vietnamese to get sick on the sudden abundance of food.

Tynan circulated among his men slowly, checking the perimeter. There was no sign that the enemy was in pursuit or that anyone was aware of their attack on the prison camp. Those who had escaped into the jungle apparently had kept running. They weren't coming back in the near future and there was no indication that anyone else was going to investigate.

With his perimeter secured, he moved back to Jones, who had managed to open the shackles, freeing the South Vietnamese from that torture. He was talking to one of them quietly in French. Two others were sitting up, eating from a single C-ration can of sliced peaches and mumbling happily and noisily.

"That a good idea?" asked Tynan.

"Couldn't hurt. I'm not going to let them have anything else. They're the strongest two."

"I mean all the noise," Tynan said.

"I'll get them to hold it down. You've got to remember that we just freed them from a prison camp."

"I understand," said Tynan, "but we're not out of the woods yet, so to speak."

"Aye, aye, sir."

"These guys going to be able to travel?"

"How far?"

"To the river, of course. Once we get there, we can get a boat to pick us up."

"How about airlift now that we've hit the camp? The V.C. know we're here."

"LZs are as far away as the river. Besides, that's exactly what the enemy is going to expect. Everyone always calls in airlift to get out. We'll beat feet for the river and fake them all out of their shorts."

"Aye, aye, sir."

Tynan glanced at his watch, surprised that only little more than an hour had passed since they had begun the attack. It seemed to have been hours, but the important thing was that it would be light in little more than two hours. That would make travel simpler, but also more dangerous.

"We'll rest here for another thirty minutes and then get moving."

Jones didn't say a word. He turned back to the South Vietnamese. They were all in bad shape. Lesions covered them. Rashes. There were open sores that leaked pus. All of them needed food and water and a great deal of rest, and none of them needed a forced hike through the jungle.

Tynan returned to the perimeter, where he took his position again, watching the vegetation in front of him, listening for sounds that the enemy was somewhere out there stalking him. The only noise was the popping of rounds cooking off in the fires on the enemy camp. No one was shooting and it didn't seem that anyone was looking for them.

After thirty minutes, Tynan called in his men. They surrounded the South Vietnamese. Callahan then took point and Tynan brought up the rear. Jones stayed with the South Vietnamese, helping a couple of them. Mathis was out as a flanker and James was on the other side. Webb was detailed to help Jones as much as he could. If they were careful, if they were quiet, they shouldn't walk into an ambush.

The pace set by Callahan was slow. He tried not to overtax the South Vietnamese but he had to avoid the jungle trails. If there was an ambush waiting anywhere, it would be on a trail. But it was no one longer important that they leave no sign. He chopped at the vines and the low-hanging branches, clearing a path for the South Vietnamese. He tried not to make noise but it was nearly impossible.

In the rear, Tynan could hear Callahan chopping his way through the jungle, but knew that the Vietnamese wouldn't be able to make it otherwise. He dropped back farther, hoping that he would be able to bail them out if they ran into trouble; hoping that he would be able to get to the rear of an ambush and break it up before it could do much damage.

But even the enforced slow pace brought sweat to his forehead and body. Some of it was the exertion of moving through the jungle and some of it was because they were surrounded by the enemy. He didn't know exactly where the enemy was hiding, but he knew they were out there. Normally it was the Vietcong and the NVA who made the noise as they patrolled, assuming that the Americans would never hear them. It was one of the reasons that Tynan and his men were able to penetrate the jungle lairs of the enemy. They moved quietly, listening for the enemy. Now it was his men making the noise and it was the enemy who would do the listening.

It became torture for Tynan. He wanted to shout at the men so that they would fall to silence. They stumbled and grunted and rattled the leaves of bushes, but it couldn't be helped. Men who had been confined to cages, who had been beaten, could not be expected to maintain the noise discipline of a well-trained, healthy outfit. They were too sick and too tired for a march through the jungle.

After forty minutes, Tynan's nerves were shot. He jumped at each sound, sure that it was the beginning of the ambush he expected. Using the small radio, he called Callahan and told him to hole up. Let the rest of the unit catch him.

Within minutes, Tynan was sitting among his men, their faces only inches from his. He whispered to them. "This is not working. If there is anyone looking for us, they're going to have no trouble finding us. We're making enough noise for a division in here."

"We could wait until it's light."

"No," said Tynan. "We need to get to the river. Callahan, you and I will go ahead, checking the way. The rest of you will laager here. If we're not back by daylight, then head for the river."

"You sure, Skipper?" asked Jones.

"It's the only thing we can do. You follow at first light," he said.

"Aye, aye, sir."

With that, Tynan moved back, away from the laager. He joined Callahan and the two of them slipped into the jungle. Now they moved faster and more quietly, Callahan no longer chopping at the vines and overhanging branches. As they headed to the river, Tynan was afraid someone was following their trail to the laager. He kept imagining that some V.C. officer had managed to get them organized.

But even with that fear, they could move no faster. The jungle was dense, holding them back. Tynan was soaked with sweat and the breath caught in his throat. He fought to control his breathing so that he didn't sound like a sick dog panting on a sun-choked porch. He didn't say a word, letting Callahan set the pace.

And then, when he was sure that he would have to call a halt, he smelled the water and heard it lapping at the banks. He caught Callahan as he crouched on the bank looking at the expanse of the river.

"I make it four clicks back to our camp."

Tynan nodded and glanced over his shoulder. "Forty or fifty minutes back but sunup in twenty or so."

"There's no one between us and the others."

Tynan grinned. "That mean you're ready to head on back there?"

"No, sir. Means that the way is clear for them. We don't have to go get them."

"Let's check this out and then we'll decide if we need to go back for the others."

Callahan nodded but didn't move. He stayed crouched among the vegetation, watching the river in front of him. Tynan understood. After a night in the jungle, with the PBR only a few minutes away if it was on call as they had been promised, it seemed ridiculous to tempt fate again by moving around. Of course, it made good sense militarily. If the enemy was near, he could ambush the PBR and then pick off the SEALS, especially now that they had to worry about the South Vietnamese. That was if the enemy knew what the plan was, which they didn't.

Still, it was something they had to do. Tynan waited for a moment, resting until his breathing evened out. Then, without a word to Callahan, he was on his feet, moving along the bank of the river. He didn't need to look back because he knew that Callahan would be doing his job and checking along the river in the opposite direction.

Tynan crept forward, watching his step so that he didn't slip into the water, although he would have welcomed the relief. It was uncomfortably hot in the jungle. Even without the sun, the heat and humidity seemed to be trapped under the thick canopy so that it didn't dissipate in the night. It hung there, making it hard to breath and nearly impossible to survive. Even in periods of rest, the uniform never dried completely, and the sweat stayed on the skin until the body was an oily, itching mess covered with rashes and the only relief was a long, hot, soapy shower and days of rest.

After he had moved several hundred meters along the bank, Tynan turned to head back. There was no evidence of the enemy anywhere around him; no sound, except for the buzz of insects and the calls of the night birds and, in the distance, the ever-present rumble of artillery and bombs and, of course, high-flying jets.

He found Callahan lying on the bank, under a giant flowering bush, his weapon pointed at the river. When he heard Tynan approaching, he looked up but didn't speak.

Tynan slid under the bush and put his lips close to Callahan's ear. "You find anything?"

"Nah, it was clear."

Tynan moved forward slightly. To the east, over a wide curve of the river, he could see the graying that marked dawn. First it was just a little whiteness that seemed to wash out the dimmest of the stars, but it crept upward until Tynan knew that the sun was coming.

Then, in the trees over them, the monkeys began to scream. They shook the trees and shrieked. Birds took off, calling to each other, and the noise built until it was impossible to hear anything. If Tynan hadn't seen the beginnings of dawn, he would have known it was close. The monkeys were better than any rooster.

Over the sound, Tynan said, his voice unnaturally loud, "We could run back now and Charlie'd never hear us. Hell, we could march a band through here."

"They'll be moving now," Callahan said, referring to Jones and the others.

"Right. Let's slip back about a click or so to guide them in."

Callahan looked at Tynan as if it was the dumbest idea he'd ever heard. He tugged at his ear and then patted his sweaty, camouflage-painted face with the sleeve of his uniform trying to dry his forehead. He shrugged as if to say, "Well, you're the boss."

Together they moved backward, away from the bush. They worked their way silently through the jungle, using the noise from the monkeys and birds to mask any sound they might make. And when the monkeys settled down, Tynan and Callahan began moving slowly again.

Thirty minutes later, they found Jones and his bunch. Tynan put Mathis out on point, pulled in the flankers and then he and Callahan took the rear guard. They moved through the jungle, making as much noise as a battalion, but there were no enemy soldiers to hear them. And the noise discipline had improved now that they could see better.

They reached the river and set up a small perimeter with the South Vietnamese in the center of it. Jones moved around it, checking on the Vietnamese and making a head count. The men were in bad shape, but they all had survived the trip from the camp to the river. Tynan then used the big radio to call for the PBR. He sat with his back to a large tree, facing the river, listening for the sound of the boat and thinking that it hadn't really been that bad. They had pulled it off and in a couple of hours they would be sitting in a club somewhere drinking a few ice-cold beers.

Jones approached, crouched in front of him, and said, "South Vietnamese were pretty talkative while we were waiting back there. Told me about life in the camp, what went on, the indoctrination. Shit, Skipper, they even had a radio so that they could listen to the news—news from Hanoi, but news none the less. The pisser was that it was loaded with information about the college riots in the World. How the people at home don't support our effort. How all they have to do is hold on until we tire of the war."

"Yeah, well, nothing we can do about that."

Jones nodded. "Well, I only bring it up because I couldn't see much propaganda value in letting the South Viets listen to troubles in the States. It's good for their own boys, keeps them fighting in the jungle because they can see a value to that fight. They can see how their sacrifice in the jungles provides for the eventual winning of the war. But it does nothing for the South."

Tynan nodded. "Good point."

"It gets better. They said that the radio was only brought out occasionally and they only heard a little of it because the propaganda broadcasts were directed at the others in the camps. At the Americans."

"There *were* no Americans in the camp," said Tynan, suddenly afraid that they had missed something in the dark.

"Not now. But there were—up until only a couple of hours before we got there. For some reason, Charlie moved them out. Had to be within a couple of hours of our arriving, if that long. Maybe only a couple of minutes."

"Shit!" Tynan said.

"Exactly."

7

For a moment no one spoke. It was as if the world had ceased to exist and everything was lost in a fine white mist not unlike that rising from the jungle around them. Nothing made any sense to him and he heard the words echoing in his head over and over again.

The Americans were moved a couple of hours before they got there.

A matter of hours. Maybe minutes. If they had seen the Americans being moved, they could have attacked then or they could have followed, taking the enemy when the time was right. If they had seen the Americans being moved, they would have had a dozen options available. Now it seemed like rescuing the Americans was an impossible task.

"We need airlift now," said Callahan. "That's the only way we can pull this off."

"Shut up," Tynan hissed, "and let me think."

"We can't waste time," protested Callahan. "They're getting away from us. Every second's delay is letting them get farther away from us."

"They've already gotten away from us," snapped Tynan. "A couple of minutes one way or the other won't make any difference."

"Skipper."

"Shut up. I need to think."

Tynan turned so that he was facing the brown water of the sluggish river. It looked almost like chocolate milk flowing across an uneven floor. He forced his eyes from it and tried to concentrate.

He had some advantages. One was that the enemy didn't know that the camp had been knocked over, so they wouldn't be pushing it. At least, they wouldn't get word of the attack for several hours, if they received it at all. They would have to move only at night and then would have to move slowly or they might give themselves away to American air power. Someone in the sky would spot them if they weren't very careful. But they would feel no pressure of pursuit.

Tynan pulled his map out and checked it again. The jungle was thick all the way to the Cambodian border—perfect territory for Charlie. It would be hard for the Americans in helicopters or airplanes to spot him. But during the day he would have to worry about American patrols and search-and-destroy missions. That would slow him.

The terrain seemed to filter toward the border. There were numerous ridges and valleys between the camp and Cambodia. There was one river valley that cut through all that. If the Vietcong stayed near it to avoid having to climb a dozen or more ridges, Tynan could find them. The valley narrowed as it approached Cambodia, making the area that had to be searched much smaller. Tynan could leapfrog ahead of the Vietcong with their American prisoners and string out along the valley floor.

The plan was beginning to come together for him. He could see it in his mind as if it had been diagrammed on a map with blue arrows and red arrows. And then, in the distance, came the low rumble of the engine of the PBR.

Callahan interrupted his thoughts and said, "Boat's on the way in."

"Get everyone organized. Make sure the Viets understand what we're about to do." Tynan got to his feet and
moved to his left, deeper into the jungle. He found Mathis
crouched there, his rifle in one hand. "I want a rear guard
in case Charlie has some thought of getting the boat."

"Aye, aye, Skipper."

"As the Viets climb on board, we'll pull back slowly
until it's time for us to board."

"No problem."

Tynan passed the instructions on to the other men and
then moved back to the riverbank in time to see the boat
coming in. It swung out in a wide, looping arc, its wake
a white froth behind it. To Tynan it looked more like a
fancy motorboat that some sportsman had painted a lousy
shade of green. All it needed was a couple of water-skiers
behind it to make the image perfect.

But the boat was ideal for the shallow-water operations
in the wide rivers in South Vietnam. There was a turret
in the front with a twin fifty mounted in it. The gunner
stood in it so that his head was barely above the side of
the boat. There was another gun mounted on the rear.
Both guns were manned. On each side, near where the
coxswain stood, were M60 machine guns, neither of
which were manned. One sailor knelt on the bow, a line
in his hand.

Jones stepped from the jungle, out onto a bare patch of
the bank so that the boat crew could see him. When they
spotted him, the boat turned, angling for him. He stepped
back into cover and waited.

As the coxswain throttled down and the boat slowed,
the man on the bow stood up. He held the line like he
wanted to throw it ashore, but at the last instant leaped
to the bank as the boat kissed the mud. He took a single
running step and fell to the ground.

He was up immediately, his fresh jungle fatigues now mud-stained and dirty. "Let's go," he said.

Jones broke cover again. He slipped down the bank until he stood on a mud flat, waiting there as the first of the Vietnamese appeared. He slung his weapon and helped them down one at a time. Then, as another of the boat's crew appeared to assist, Jones lifted the Vietnamese up as the crewman grabbed their hands, hauling them on board.

As he lifted one of the Vietnamese up on board, the crewman looked over and saw the line of them coming from the jungle. "Christ!" he said. "How many of them are there?"

"Thirteen."

"Fucking lucky number."

"You don't know the half of it."

They got the rest of the Vietnamese on board. Jones then climbed up and whistled once, a shrill, piercing sound. At that moment, Callahan and Mathis came out of the jungle together and leaped to the bow of the boat. As they did, the coxswain reversed the engines and begin backing off the mud before the boat became too heavy.

Tynan and James escorted Webb out of the jungle then. Webb looked panic-stricken, as if he believed he was going to be left behind. Tynan jumped to the mud, stumbled, and put out a hand to break his fall. He stood up, moved to the water's edge, and waded out toward the boat. Jones waved a hand at him and pulled him up onto the boat as Callahan helped Webb up on the other side and James followed. Tynan turned and surveyed the jungle behind them but saw no sign of the enemy.

When they were all on board, Tynan having taken a quick head count, he yelled, "That's everyone."

As the coxswain spun the wheel, taking them toward the center of the river, Tynan asked, "You got a radio?"

"Of course, sir. What do you need?"

"We need to get these guys on shore somewhere so they can be debriefed and then I've got to get another mission scheduled right away."

As the boat roared through the water, Tynan was on the radio trying to raise Clafin. Failing that, he tried to find someone with the authority to authorize a mission to the Cambodian border, but that couldn't be done either. Everyone wanted Tynan to report to them so that they could ask questions, plot information on maps and charts, and file reports. Tynan finally gave up in disgust. Jones took over then, requesting medical assistance for a number of people, all Vietnamese nationals. His request was approved and he was told that the medical assistance would be provided at the first base they could land at.

Tynan turned then and watched as they leaped through the water, the boat bouncing in the slight waves of the river. Finally, ahead of them he could see a base. There was a dock that extended out into the river and barbed wire that seemed to grow out of the water. There were sandbagged bunkers to guard the approaches from both the water and the land, and sandbagged buildings crouched in the deep greens of the trees. Some of it had been cut back for a clear killing zone.

The coxswain headed straight for the dock. As he neared, three men ran out onto it, each of them carrying a stretcher. Behind them were a couple of ambulances all painted OD green with large red crosses on them. Drivers stood near them as did a couple of people in white coats. Two helicopters circled overhead as if waiting for word to land.

As the boat eased toward the dock, several more men came forward. One of them stood there, reaching out as if waiting for a line. As soon as the boat was secured, a transfer of the Vietnamese from the deck of the boat to the dock began. As they stepped from the boat, the doctors and nurses hurried forward. Suddenly, confusion raged on the dock. One of the ambulances backed up onto it and several people had to scramble out of its way. Two men were yanking at an empty stretcher yelling at one another. Two of the Vietnamese tried to wander ashore but were turned back. One man was put on a stretcher and carried away.

Webb moved across the deck of the boat and watched as some of the Vietnamese were lifted to the dock. He stood watching and then said to Tynan, "Guess that's about it."

"Your job has been completed now," Tynan said.

Webb looked at him for an instant. "All our jobs have been completed."

"Yes, well," responded Tynan. He knew that Webb had listened to everything that the men had said, had listened as they debated the possibility of finding the Americans being held prisoner. Webb was a complication that Tynan didn't want to deal with. If he could get him onto the shore, they could leave him there wondering what in the hell was going on.

Tynan wiped a hand across his face and said, "We'll want to brief your people about the results of the raid. That's about the first thing we want to do."

"You're not going after them, are you?"

Tynan stared into Webb's eyes. He could lie to the man, but doubted he would believe it. He decided to tell the truth about it.

"Yeah, we're going to give it a try. But I need to operate with men who are trained in this kind of thing."

"I've been to the schools—"

"Listen, Webb, I don't give a shit about what training you've had. You haven't been through the right training and you haven't spent enough time in the field. I want experienced men that I can count on.''

Webb was going to object but then he looked into Tynan's eyes. He knew what Tynan meant. A survival school in Panama wasn't the same as experience in the field. ''Maybe I'll go ashore here and see if I can learn anything from the South Vietnamese we freed.''

''You do that.''

''Good luck.''

''Thanks.'' Tynan turned and watched until all the Vietnamese were on the dock. As soon as they were taken care of, he turned on the coxswain. ''I've got a problem, Chief, and I'm going to need your help if I'm going to solve it.''

The man folded his arms and leaned back, his hip resting on the wheel. He was an older man, nearing forty. There was a stubble of beard on his fleshy face and there were bags under his bloodshot eyes. There was a network of broken blood vessels on his nose that, when coupled with the beer belly, suggested a man liked to drink, and who had been drinking for the greater part of his life. His fatigues were sweat-stained and dirty. Tynan knew that the man had gone on duty at dusk, patrolling the river, waiting for his call.

''Yes, sir?'' he said.

''I need someone to take me back upriver quite a ways,'' said Tynan. ''Take most of the day to do it right.''

''Yes, sir?'' repeated the chief.

Tynan stared at him, waiting, but when the man didn't speak, Tynan said, ''We've got an indication that some American POWs are being moved. We want to intercept them. If we do it right, we might be able to get them away from the enemy.''

The expression on the chief's face changed. He nodded and asked, "Why didn't you say so before? What exactly do you need from us?"

"We need a ride upriver, nearly to Cambodia. If you've any supplies, C-rats, ammo, anything like that, we might need that too."

"You just ask, sir, you've got it. When would you like to leave?"

"Just as soon as you can get the clearance."

The man reached into the top pocket of his fatigue jacket and took out a cigar. He didn't light it. He chomped on it for a moment and then said, "Hell, Lieutenant, I've got all the clearance I need. If you're ready, we'll get going."

Tynan looked at his men. He wanted them all to have a say in this because this part of the mission wasn't exactly authorized. It was a logical follow-up to their last mission and if he could contact Clafin, he could probably get approval. He didn't think there would be any negative ramifications, but you couldn't tell. Sometimes the brass went ape-shit over things like this, especially when they began operating close to Cambodia. But then, there wasn't time for a long debate about it. If he was going to pull it off, he had to move quickly.

"Let's get going," said Tynan. He laid his map out where the chief could see it. "When we get into this area here, I want to begin looking for a place for us to go ashore."

"Aye, aye, sir. Be a couple of hours for us to get that far up there."

"Then let's do it."

The chief turned back and started the engines. As he did, one of his crewmen cast off the lines and they worked their way back into the middle of the channel.

Tynan moved to the stern and motioned to his men. As they gathered around him, he spread his map out on the deck, holding it down so that the wind wouldn't rip it off into the river. He looked into the grimy, dirty, camo-smeared faces of his men and wondered if he was doing the right thing.

"All right, men, here's the deal. The terrain in the area suggests that the enemy is going to cross into Cambodia in the valley near this river. I think we can find them because they'll be taking the easy route. No reason for them to get fancy at this point. I haven't been able to get any kind of authorization for this mission, but I don't think we'll have trouble about it afterwards."

"Why are you telling us all this, Skipper?" asked Jones, grinning.

Tynan looked at the young man, who still had camouflage paint smeared on his face so thick that it was impossible to tell a thing about him. His uniform was ripped in a couple of places and he could have used a shower.

"Well," said Tynan, "I wanted you all to know that I was getting this thing going without clearing it with higher headquarters. I thought it was only fair to warn you that we could catch some flak."

"And if we free those men," said Callahan, "we could catch a couple of medals."

"We're not going after medals," said Tynan.

"I know that, Skipper. What I mean is, it's one of those things you don't know about. Maybe the brass will reward us for a little initiative, rather than stepping on us for it."

"Okay," said Tynan, "here's what I want to do." He carefully outlined the plan as he saw it. They would all have to work separately, outside of close support from one another. Since they had no clearances, they would have to be careful they didn't blunder into an American ambush or get hit by American aircraft because no one knew they were there. And if they stepped into it, they would play hell trying to get close air support or army aviation to pick them up. They would be on their own.

"Don't worry about it, Skipper. If we pull it off, it'll be worth it."

Tynan nodded. That was how he felt about it, too. If they freed the Americans, it would be more than worth it.

Tynan stretched out on the deck of the boat, used a boonie hat to cover his eyes, and tried to catch some sleep. He had been awake for over thirty hours without much sleep. Now was the only chance that he would have to catch any, and although he knew that he should be studying the map or checking the equipment, he needed the rest.

He slept for a while. Then he rolled to his side and put a hand out. The deck was hot to the touch and he was covered with sweat. He began to breath rapidly and wished that he could get out of the direct rays of the sun, but that was impossible. The deck space was limited and the only cover was over the coxswain.

Tynan managed to rest for a while anyway. The rumbling of the boat's engine and the vibrations on the deck were comforting. He listened to the engine, trying to exclude the sounds of the war in the distance.

Finally he sat up. He wiped a hand on the back of his neck and studied the sweat on it. It looked like he had been in swimming. His fatigue jacket was soaked and looked black. He got to his feet and moved to the shade of the canopy over the coxswain.

"I make it another hour or so, sir," said the chief without waiting for the question.

"You got anything cold to drink?"

The chief grinned and said, "What? You think we're the marines? Of course we've got something cold to drink. Hold on to the wheel and I'll get you a beer."

Tynan stepped around the chief and grabbed the wheel, blinking into the bright sunlight as it reflected off the dirty water. He kept the boat in the center of the river and didn't touch the throttles.

The jungle flashed by in a green blur. Some of the vegetation came to the water's edge, growing out of it and hiding the bank. Trees leaned over it, their branches dipping into the muddy water. A snake of some kind dropped from a branch into the river and slithered off along the shore.

The chief touched his shoulder and then held the can in front of his face. The sides were beaded with moisture. "You want me to open it for you?"

"I can get it."

"Thought you were enjoying yourself, sir. Thought maybe you'd like to keep the helm for a while."

Tynan was going to shake his head and then decided what the hell. It gave him something to do, took his mind off the coming mission. "Yeah," he said. "Go ahead and open it."

He took the can and held it against his forehead. Then he drank from it, surprised that the beer was so cold. He thought it would shatter his teeth and he felt it as it pooled in his stomach, numbing the muscles. He glanced at the chief in surprise.

"We have access to a lot of spare equipment and we adapt some of it for our use."

Tynan drained the beer and handed the can back to the chief. He had been going to throw it over the side, but had remembered the booby traps he'd seen: grenades stuck into cans. Why give Charlie any help?

"You want to take over, Chief?"

"You're doing fine, Lieutenant."

"Yeah, but I should brief my men. We can't be too far from our destination."

"No, sir, not all that far now. How did you want to handle this?"

Tynan reached up and wiped his face again. "Seems to me that if you put into shore once, Charlie, if he's around, is going to know right where we are and what is happening. I think we'll want to touch the bank in several places so that if anyone is watching, or listening, we might confuse them. He'll still know that a patrol came ashore, but he won't know who or where, if we're lucky."

"Going ashore in the daylight like that, I doubt we'll fool anyone who's out there to watch."

"Still, why make it easy for him?"

"Aye, aye, sir."

"Once we're off the boat I'd like you to continue on for a click or so before turning around. Then you can race right back down the river without a hesitation. If there are any free fire zones on your route, you might want to put some rounds into them for the hell of it."

The chief moved in and took the wheel. Tynan took another look at the river and then said, "I'll make the chart for you."

"Not necessary, sir. Just point it out and I'll put you on shore."

"When you get back to your base, you might want to contact Commander Richard Clafin. Talk to him in person and let him know where we are, more or less. Let him know why we've gone back into the field."

"Aye, aye, sir."

Tynan stood there for a moment longer and then stepped around onto the stern of the boat. He nodded to

Jones and waved him over. One by one the rest of the team joined them.

They settled down and Tynan said, "Once we're on land, we're going to be spread pretty thin. We'll use the same codes on the radio that we've used for the last week, but I doubt that the man farthest right will be in touch with the one on the left. We'll have to relay until we locate the patrol and then draw in."

He stopped talking, studied the map, and then looked at the men. "Anyone have any questions?" It was a fairly straightforward patrol with little chance for success unless Tynan had made a number of right guesses.

The men were quiet, studying the map. They had no questions for him.

"Then let's get ready to go ashore." He stood and moved back to the chief, showing him where he wanted to go ashore.

"I think that's a couple of clicks ahead. I'll start the diversions now."

"Thanks, Chief."

"Say, Lieutenant, give 'em hell for me, will you?"

"Sure."

"I'll signal you when it's time for you to hit the beach, so to speak."

"Thanks." Tynan returned to his men. He couched and checked his weapon, making sure it was on safe. Carefully, he went over the equipment he carried, checking it. The three canteens dragged at the pistol, making him feel heavy. He wanted to take another drink of water, no matter how hot it was, and wished that he had time for another beer, but put it all out of his mind. Now he had to concentrate on the mission in front of him, not the creature comforts he was denied.

He heard the pitch in the engines change as the boat suddenly turned toward the closest bank. As they slowed, he wanted to say, "This is it," but it was a cliché from a hundred war movies. Everyone always said that just before the big invasion. This wasn't a big invasion. Just a small squad going ashore to tangle with a few V.C. Maybe. Instead, he told his men, "This is a diversion. Be another ten, fifteen minutes."

8

On the third run in to the shore, Tynan and his team were ready. The chief spotted a gap in the thick vegetation that lined the banks of the river and aimed for it. One of the crewmen, lying on the bow of the boat so that he could be sure that they didn't run aground, guided them in. As they turned to head back out, Tynan and his men leaped from the deck. All of them dropped into the shallow water so that there were no footprints on the banks. As the boat turned and raced toward the center of the river, they began moving along the bank, searching for a good place to enter the jungle.

Jones found it a moment later. The vegetation was back away from the water and the ground dipped down close to the surface of the river. By grabbing the exposed root of a tree, Jones could haul himself out of the knee-deep water. As soon as he was up out of the water, he saw very little evidence that they had come ashore there and after the sun dried the ground, there would be none at all.

They moved inland rapidly. Once they were three hundred meters from the river, Tynan stopped them again. He pulled out his map and tried to orient himself with the few landmarks that were visible to him. He knew what the river looked like as they approached and had seen the mouth of a small tributary not far away. There were the remains of a small bridge that had been destroyed by the enemy months before. With three good landmarks, Tynan was sure that he knew where they were. Given the time frame, he was sure that he was between the American prisoners and the Cambodian border. The real question was whether or not he had guessed right. If not, then it didn't matter where they were.

He folded his map and stuffed it back into his pocket. He sat on the ground for a moment, a damp, thick padding of rotting vegetation under him, then looked up into the sweating faces of his men. Now that he was into the jungle, he didn't like to talk. He didn't want to make any unnecessary noise, but he needed to give them a few instructions. Although he had told them on the boat that he wanted them to spread out north to south along the valley floor, now that he was into the field again, he had convinced himself that his men wouldn't know what to do. There were just some things that he wouldn't take for granted.

The mission wasn't an active one. All they had to do was spread out so that they could cover the largest area and communicate with the line-of-sight radios. They had to sit patiently and let the enemy come to them. Nothing to it. Still he hesitated, feeling that it was a fool's mission. To find one specific unit of the V.C. by leaping ahead of them seemed impossible—especially when he wasn't sure what their destination was or when they had left or what their route of march was. He had to guess where they were going and the route they would take. Talk about needles in haystacks.

But there was nothing to do but get on with it. Tynan spoke quietly so that even he could barely hear the words. He told the men to spread out. Jones would anchor right where they were, only a few hundred meters from the river. Callahan would move another couple of hundred meters. Then James and Mathis and finally Tynan. With luck, they would be spread over little more than a click with Tynan at the base of the hills. They would have to rely on their ears and senses more than their eyes, alert for any changes in the jungle around them. Maybe the monkeys would suddenly start fleeing, or maybe scream at one another without the provocation of sunup. Maybe the jungle birds would suddenly burst into flight. Or maybe some of the giant fruit bats hanging in the trees would awaken and fly. Whatever it was, they would have to be alert and check it out because it would mean a change on the ground.

The men knelt near him and nodded their agreement. They all knew exactly what had to be done. When he had finished, Tynan stood and told them to move out. With James, Mathis, and Callahan, he left Jones behind. They moved through the jungle slowly, figuring they had plenty of time. The last thing they wanted was to be seen by enemy scouts who would then turn the tables on them. Instead of chopping their way through the thickest part of the jungle, they worked around it or under it. They didn't want anyone to be able to see they had been there or be able to guess where they were going.

It took them twenty minutes to move a hundred meters and then nearly an hour to move another hundred. Callahan dropped off then, crawling back into a thicket. Once he was in it, even Tynan, nearly standing on top of him, couldn't see him. Satisfied that Callahan was well hidden, Tynan, Mathis, and James moved out.

In forty minutes they found the perfect place for James. He hid himself, and Tynan and Mathis continued on until they noticed that the ground was beginning to slope slightly upward. He told Mathis to backtrack twenty meters or so and find a place to hide. Tynan would keep going. He knew they had reached the edge of the valley. He climbed up the hillside and began searching for a place to hide. It took him ten minutes to find the perfect place, but the one he found was nearly ideal. He had a good view for several hundred meters in front of him and if anyone came between him and the top of the ridge, he was sure to see them.

Once he was settled, he used the radio to contact James to alert him that all was set. He had to point the antenna of the tiny radio in James's direction, but he got a whispered response. James passed the word down the line and in moments relayed a message back that no one had seen anything.

He then contacted Mathis to make sure that he was in position. Mathis didn't answer verbally. He merely broke squelch, letting Tynan know that he had received the message.

Tynan crept back into the bush and stretched out prone. The radio was turned low and right next to his ear. His rifle was in his hands and one of his canteens sat close by. Then he settled down, frozen in place but keeping his eyes in motion, watching the ground around him as he listened for someone to approach.

He was back out of the sun, but it was still hot and muggy. The air, trapped under the dense canopy of the jungle, didn't circulate. It settled to the ground threatening to smother him. It was an almost visible force that drifted through the trees, oppressing everything around it. Overhead, in the upper reaches of the canopy, he could hear a breeze, but the thick, interlocked branches of the trees prevented its reaching down into the jungle.

Even lying there, not exerting himself, he was hot. He felt the sweat on his body, dripping down his face and sides, but now he refused to move to wipe it away. When lying in wait, you didn't move; you tried not to breath; you tried not to think about what you were doing. Movement and failure to concentrate were the quickest ways to give yourself away. Tynan had seen it happen a dozen times. He had crouched on hillsides and in jungles, searching the surroundings for the enemy who invariably moved.

So he lay there quietly, listening to the sounds of the jungle around him. Listening to the calls of the animals and the birds and the noise the monkeys made as they played in the tops of the trees. He listened to the sounds of the insects as they searched for food, the sound of the flies: buzzing that at times seemed so loud that it could drown out the sound of a firefight close to him.

And there was the smell. It was a musty, dirty odor like dirt that was mildewing. Maybe it was the smell of a grave. He drove that thought from his mind because the last thing that a soldier on ambush needed to think about was the inside of a grave.

After an hour there was a quiet pop from the radio. It was Mathis telling him that everything was all clear. He hoped that Mathis had waited for the signal from Callahan and James so that it meant that everything was clear up and down the line. It was the thing that he hated the most. Not being in direct contact with the far end of his line, but it couldn't be helped. He wanted radios with a limited range so that the enemy, if he happened to be monitoring the radio, wouldn't be able to pick up the signals.

He put that out of his mind, too, and watched the jungle in front of him. He was amazed at the size of some of the insects: huge beetles six or seven inches long, poisonous centipedes over a foot long, and a spider that was even larger; giant insects that ignored him because he was lying so quietly. He kept his eye on the centipede until it disappeared, moving away from him, and even after it was gone he was sure that he could hear it moving through the thick, damp vegetation.

Finally he turned slightly and drank some of his water; it was warm and tasted of plastic and halazone. It helped, even though what he really wanted was a cold beer. He had intended to eat, but just didn't feel like it, so he ignored his hunger and concentrated on the sounds around him.

Just as he decided that he would finally have something to eat, he heard a rustling in the jungle in front of him. He froze, letting his eyes search. He caught a flicker of movement for an instant, but couldn't pin it down. It might have been an animal, for all he knew. He waited patiently and it came again: it was human.

He strained his senses, but whoever it was didn't want to be seen. Then there was more movement and he spotted him. He watched the man, dressed in black pajamas with a pouch on his chest for the spare banana clips of an AK-47, turn, heading straight for him—a Vietnamese wearing Ho Chi Minh sandals and carrying an AK.

Tynan watched the man and decided that he was well trained but not searching for anyone. He was on a routine patrol as point man. Tynan touched his radio and signaled the men with him that an enemy soldier was near. Again he hoped that Mathis and James had the good sense to relay the message. With that finished, he didn't move again.

The enemy came closer, edging around the thickest of the brush, dodging the obstacles. It seemed that he had seen Tynan was coming right at him. For a moment Tynan almost panicked, afraid that he had somehow given himself away, but then realized that the man didn't look like he had spotted an enemy soldier. He kept his pace steady and his eyes roaming.

He was now close enough that Tynan could see that his feet were dirty. He had a makeshift pistol belt with a metal canteen on it. For the souvenir hunters in Saigon the man was a walking trophy case—a couple of hundred dollars of enemy equipment.

Just when it seemed that the V.C. would walk right up to Tynan, he turned slightly, searching for the valley floor. As that man passed out of sight, more of them appeared. It was a squad-sized unit that had put out a point and maintained noise discipline, but didn't bother with flankers. They were all V.C. Not one of them wore the khaki of the NVA.

Tynan waited patiently, looking for signs that they had American prisoners with them, but the Americans never showed. Besides, the unit didn't look like prison guards. These men were very good in the bush, making almost no noise. They didn't walk with their weapons on their shoulders and they didn't bunch up. They weren't talking or playing grab-ass or smoking. They stayed spread out, each man concentrating on the jungle around him as they patrolled.

Tynan was sure that he could have taken them, if they had been the right people. One by one, his men could attack the rear of the squad, using their knives, until they had killed them all. But that wasn't the purpose of the mission. He wished there were some way to take them, but couldn't think of how to do it without compromising his own position. If too many V.C. disappeared, they would figure out that an American patrol was around.

When the last of the enemy soldiers was out of sight and he could hear nothing more of them, he waited another ten minutes before signaling the all-clear. Then he relaxed and waited in the hot environment, wishing again that he had a cold beer, a hot steak, and a woman who was interested in his body and not his mind.

He passed the rest of the day there, waiting, watching, and listening. Once he rolled onto his side to relieve himself, being careful that he didn't foul his hiding place.

And he spent ten minutes sequentially flexing his muscles to relieve the stiffness caused by enforced inactivity. He had to be careful because he didn't want to make any unnecessary movements that might give him away.

The night arrived suddenly. One minute it was bright, the next it was dim, and then it was dark. There was very little to the dusk. The sounds around him changed then. The noise from the animals was different as the nocturnal beasts came out to hunt for their food. The insects stopped buzzing as night fell, then they started up again. Gnats swarmed around his head, darting at his eyes, but Tynan couldn't swat at them. The jungle was a noisy place, alive with motion as the animals who hid during the heat and humidity of the day came out into the heat and humidity of the night.

With a covering of darkness intensified to a near pitch blackness by the dense jungle canopy, Tynan crawled from his cover. He stood up slowly, listening to the muscles and joints pop as he stretched. He stood still for a moment and listened. Then he drank deeply from one of his canteens. Given their distance from the prison camp, he didn't think that the enemy could get to his position during the night. It would be the next day at the earliest. That meant he probably should sleep during this night and plan to stay awake all of the next. The thing was, he didn't know if he should pull in his line so that each man would have a partner.

Finally he picked up his radio and told Mathis that he would be moving in closer so that they could support one another. He gave the same message to James and told James to relay the message and have Callahan and Jones pair up for the night.

He picked up his equipment and moved back toward the river. He found James and Mathis and joined them. They set up a schedule of watches so that one man could sleep for four or five hours without interruption. Tynan took the first watch while James and Mathis crawled under a bush to sleep.

It was a funny thing, thought Tynan. In the jungle, on patrol, he never heard anyone snore. In camp, surrounded by wire and hundreds of other Americans, the same men would sound like participants at a lumberjack convention where everyone had to try out his new chain saw. But here, where the slightest sound could mean instant death, no one snored.

The hours passed quickly, which puzzled Tynan. Hours in the bush, watching the blackness of a jungle, usually passed like days in a boring classroom, moving so slowly that he could understand the concept of eternity. But James was suddenly next to him, telling him it was his turn for the watch. It seemed as though only minutes had passed.

Tynan crawled under the bush and rolled to his side. He couldn't sleep on his back in the jungle. He had a dread that he would sleep with his mouth open and something would fall into it—a poisonous plant, an insect . . . something. He just couldn't do it. So he rolled to his side, put an arm under his head, and tried to go to sleep.

And in minutes, it seemed, Mathis, who had taken over for James, was trying to wake him. Tynan came out of his dreams slowly, at first unsure of where he was. Then he remembered suddenly and was shocked by his inability to focus faster than he had. He told himself it was because he subconsciously knew that he was in no danger. Still, it was a frightening thing for a combat soldier to have done.

With the coming of morning, Tynan spread the men out for another day in the jungle. As he moved into his position, he took some Dexedrine, washing it down with warm water. Then he settled in, secure in the knowledge that he wouldn't fall asleep during the inactivity of the day.

It was a repeat of the day before, but now, with the Dexedrine pumping through him, he heard and saw more, his senses heightened by the drug. He was more aware of everything that was going on around him.

At midmorning, the jungle glowing green around him, he heard a rumbling overhead that was not bombs or artillery. The jungle filled with what sounded like bacon frying; it was the rain, but the jungle canopy was so thick that the water wasn't reaching the ground. He listened to the storm over him and wondered if it would make Charlie move faster. The rain would inhibit the American aviation assets, keeping them grounded. Charlie could make up for lost time if he didn't mind getting wet.

The storm moved on and the sound diminished. After nearly an hour, the plants began to drip as the water from the top level of the canopy seeped downward, from leaf to leaf to a trunk of a tree to the lacy branches of the ferns. Although the storm was over, Tynan was just beginning to get wet from it. He listened to the sound of it filtering through the jungle, making noise as large leaves filled with water and then turned over, making it sound like someone was sneaking up had slipped, falling to the ground.

The rainwater soaked Tynan completely, making him more aware of the itching on his body from the days of sweating without a chance to shower. It wasn't a refreshing feeling, either; it made him miserable. And to make it worse, the clouds overhead thinned and vanished, letting the sunlight through to bake the upper levels of the canopy. The whole jungle began to steam, and with no outlets for the humidity, it became oppressively hard to breathe.

Through all that, Tynan and his team remained silent. Tynan made one radio check as the water began to reach the ground to make sure that the radios still worked. Both Mathis and James acknowledged his call. The radios were operating.

At noon, there was a normal radio check. Again, Tynan heard nothing from Jones and Callahan. He barely heard James but Mathis came through loud and clear. So far everything was going just as it was supposed to.

Late in the afternoon, the radio came alive again. James whispered into it that he thought that Callahan was telling them that someone was coming. Mathis acknowledged that he heard. Tynan tensed and waited but nothing else was forthcoming. He began to wonder if Callahan had been found and captured, but realized that Callahan would not be taken without firing a shot or two. If he wasn't making any other radio transmissions, it meant that the enemy was still close to him. Callahan wouldn't want to risk the movement to make a radio call when he had nothing new to report.

And Tynan had no idea what Jones was doing on the other side of Callahan. Tynan could only hope that Jones had heard the message and was lying low until the enemy force moved on out of the region.

Tynan wanted to crawl closer, but he wasn't sure about the enemy positions. Callahan hadn't given them a report on the disposition of the patrol. He had let them know that the enemy was close to him and then fallen silent. Without more information, anything Tynan did might be a mistake. All he could do was wait until Callahan let him know what was going on or made a call asking for help. Again he needed to be patient.

And then the call came—James relaying that Callahan had reported the enemy unit moving to west northwest in a column formation. He had watched them as they took a break no more than twenty meters from him, listening to them talk quietly. They had shared a quick lunch of rice balls and water from their canteens. As they moved out, he had spotted one white man wearing ripped dirty fatigues, obviously an American. A moment later another appeared, followed closely by the rear guard. Callahan counted fifteen guards with the Americans, but there could have been a couple he hadn't seen.

James asked, "What do we do?"

"Everyone draw toward the center and pick up the trail. We begin following them until we can get close enough to assess the situation."

There were no verbal responses. Just a series of clicks on the radio as the men acknowledged the orders. When he knew that his men had gotten his orders, Tynan crawled from his cover, and began to angle through the jungle. He knew that the enemy would be following the path that meandered through the bottom of the valley about three hundred meters from the river. It was exactly the path that he had envisioned them taking. The map had made it obvious that the enemy would be in this valley, moving more or less toward the Cambodian border. For some reason, he wasn't surprised that they had found the right patrol or that he had predicted their probable path with such accuracy. He took it in stride.

9

With very little coordination, Tynan's men pulled together in the center of the valley. Callahan ended up on point because he had been the closest to the enemy when they had passed. Jones was next, then James, and finally Mathis. Tynan fell in at the rear of the formation. He hadn't needed help from anyone to find the path because the V.C. weren't bothering with trying to disguise their route of march. They were heading for Cambodia rapidly.

The SEALS stayed with it, matching the speed of the enemy patrol, but forced to maintain noise discipline, which hindered them slightly. Callahan, at point, had visual contact with the VC, and therefore was in command. He used his radio to give the orders, relying on the coded clicks they had used on the earlier mission.

Tynan hung back as far as he dared, listening for the sounds of a second patrol following the first. Since the camp had been attacked, he wondered if some of the survivors might not be trying to catch the men who had left earlier, but he heard and saw nothing. There were no indications that the V.C. suspected that the SEALS were following.

Late in the afternoon, they broke out of the thick jungle vegetation. The triple canopy that had blocked the sun gave way to a sporadic canopy riddled with holes. The surroundings brightened considerably, forcing Callahan to retreat so that he wouldn't be seen by the Vietcong.

Because of the added sun, it now seemed hotter, as if sunlamps had been introduced to the sauna. Within a couple hundred meters, all the men were soaked through, their breathing now raspy. They had to fight the tendency to pant, so that they didn't betray their presence to the enemy.

Just as Tynan started to believe that they couldn't continue, the V.C. halted in a copse of trees that had a thick canopy to protect them from the prying eyes of American air power. They spread out in a circular formation with the American prisoners held in the middle. They stacked some of their weapons and broke out a cooking pot. One man dug a shallow hole and another arranged a series of palm leaves above it as a third began building a fire. The palm leaves dissipated the smoke so that no one would be able to see it as it filtered upward.

As they arranged their camp, Callahan slipped back deeper into the jungle. He whispered his observations into the radio and waited for further instructions. Twenty minutes later the whole team was gathered.

Callahan didn't wait for Tynan to start the debriefing. He whispered, "They seem to be making camp for the night."

"How can you be sure?" Tynan asked.

"They've built a fire and they're cooking a meal. They've posted a couple of guards and one or two of them seem to be gathering palm leaves for beds."

"How are they positioned?"

Callahan rocked forward and scraped some of the rotting leaves from the ground. With a stick he drew a loose circle in the soft earth.

"Okay, they've got a perimeter out with five or six guys on it. We're here, to the south and west, with maybe two guys in our way. Others are posted here and here. In the middle, they have a cooking pot and three or four guys who have stacked their arms. Right near them, with three guards watching them like hawks, are the Americans.''

Tynan studied the drawing. ''There's no way we can just sneak in and grab them now. Too many people watching. Too many people awake.''

''If we wait, they may press on. Head straight to Cambodia. That's what I'd do.''

Tynan nodded. ''But the problem is they've been on the go most of the afternoon. I suspect they'll stay here for the night and begin again early tomorrow morning. They've no reason to suspect that we're back here.''

''Skipper, it seems to me that they'd continue on until midnight and then camp.''

''Makes no difference,'' said Tynan. ''If they pull out, we follow. If they don't, we hit them right here.'' He plucked the stick out of Callahan's grasp and added, ''We go in through here. Take out these two guards quietly, move into the camp, kill the guards watching our men, and then exfiltrate the way we came in. Quickly and quietly. Use the claymores as a mechanical rear guard.''

''Unless they move.''

''Shit!'' snapped Tynan. ''If they move, they'll probably set up the new camp in much the same way. We'll hit it as soon as we have the guards identified and they have a chance to settle down.''

''Sure, Skipper.''

Tynan looked at the tired, sweaty faces of the men. ''Okay, I think we need to get some rest ourselves. I want one man to move in on their camp; he can watch it, so that if they move we won't be caught flat-footed. If they don't take off, we'll pull back about midnight, give them an hour, and hit them about two in the morning.''

Tynan glanced at each of the men again. When they said nothing, he pointed to Callahan. The younger man turned and began working his way through the bush again, back to the enemy camp. He moved slowly, as if crippled, but made no noise. When the camp was close, he stopped and waited.

Without speaking, Tynan formed them into a loose circle. One man with the main body kept an eye on Callahan, who was the scout. The other two men could relax slightly, drink water, eat a cold, slow meal of C-rations, or just lie still. Every thirty minutes they rotated the duty so that everyone got a chance to eat and rest whether they wanted it or not.

Now the time did pass slowly. While Tynan was outside the circle, watching the enemy camp, it got completely dark. As the last of the light faded, the V.C. put out their fire, realizing that at night the glow from the flames was more dangerous than the smoke in the day.

Although they were only fifty meters from him, he heard almost nothing from their camp. They maintained their noise discipline as effectively as did Tynan's SEALS. Once he heard a quiet discussion between an officer and an enlisted man but that was it. The V.C. rotated their duties frequently, giving no one man a chance to really fuck up.

Watching them showed Tynan he was dealing with well-disciplined, but average soldiers. Those who weren't on some kind of guard duty stacked their weapons. If they weren't eating or drinking, they were sleeping. Only the men who were actively guarding either the perimeter or the Americans seemed to be alert, and as Tynan studied them, he noticed that they were beginning to doze off, too.

He rotated his position outside the circle to Jones, but set it up so that he had the last look at the enemy camp.

He studied it as best he could, now that it was night. He could tell that the majority of the men were asleep. There was a skeleton guard and one man who kept an eye on the Americans.

Finally he decided he had seen enough. He crawled to the rear and found his men. They drew back until they were face to face. He could hear their breathing, felt their foul breath on his face, and he could smell them, but he couldn't actually see them. They were just black shapes against a blacker background.

In careful, quiet whispers they discussed exactly what they were going to do. Callahan and Mathis would lead. They would creep forward, find the two closest guards, and kill them. James and Jones would follow Tynan as he moved forward. It was Tynan's job to kill the guard watching the Americans. James and Jones would cover him and then guard his retreat. After Callahan and Mathis had killed their guards, they would fade back to set up the mechanical rear guard. They all would then retreat the way they had come, heading first to the south and east and then toward the river.

After the briefing, they stashed their rucksacks, hiding them in the jungle in case they couldn't get back for them. They left the large radio with that equipment. Finally ready, Tynan nodded, and Callahan and Mathis started forward moving as slowly as they had to. They could afford no noise at all.

Five minutes after they moved out, Tynan started off with Jones and James right behind him. He walked the first fifty meters hunched over, his hands close to the ground, but as he neared the enemy perimeter, he got down onto his belly. He slung his rifle, fastening it down so that it wouldn't make noise. He pulled his knife as he began to crawl.

He didn't bother to look back. Jones and James had to be behind him. He couldn't hear them as they all moved forward slowly and carefully. At one point he heard a soft, quiet moan close by. He raised up and saw the sandaled foot of one of the guards just after he had died. Either Callahan or Mathis had completed the first part of his mission.

Tynan kept moving, hand out in front, first one foot and then the other, until he got a rhythm going. He slipped through the thin grass and between the low bushes. He stopped once, glanced up, and saw that the guard on the American prisoners was sitting facing the opposite direction. His head was bowed as if he had gone to sleep.

Tynan began moving again. He crept to within a few feet of the enemy soldier, slowly getting up so that he was crouched behind the man. In a single motion, he grabbed the man under the chin, jerking his head up. As the man's eyes snapped open, Tynan struck with his knife. He cut the enemy's throat as he dragged the man backward. He then jammed the knife upward, over the right kidney, twisting it as it penetrated the enemy soldier's back. He felt him spasm once, going completely rigid. Then he collapsed as he died. Tynan laid the body down in the deep grass, the odor of the man's death unmistakable.

Tynan glanced to the rear and saw that both Jones and James were covering him. He moved forward toward the sleeping shapes of the Americans. He stopped short and looked at the men, barely visible in the darkness of the jungle.

He crouched over one of them, reaching out to put a hand over the man's mouth so that he wouldn't cry out in surprise as he woke. But as he moved toward the American, the man rolled over, his eyes wide open. He

glanced at Tynan but remained silent. There was no surprise in his eyes or on his face. Just a curiosity that asked,
"What took so long?"

Tynan stepped beyond him and found that the second
man was awake, too. He helped the man sit up and then
used his knife to cut the hobble that had been tied around
the man's ankles. As that prisoner struggled to his knees,
Tynan cut the ropes on the first man. He didn't speak to
either of them. They knew exactly what was happening.

When he had freed them both, he turned, heading back
into the night with the two men behind him. He moved
very carefully, afraid of alerting the sleeping enemy soldiers. Reaching James and Jones, he had them help the
two freed Americans. With that, they picked up the pace,
working their way through the makeshift perimeter.

In only minutes they reached the positions held by
Mathis and Callahan. As he approached them, Mathis
touched his shoulder and put his lips next to Tynan's ear.

"We've got trouble, Skipper."

"What?"

"There's someone behind us. Someone moving into the
area. Heard them a couple of times but haven't seen anyone. From the sound of it though, there has to be quite
a few of them. I don't think they're Americans."

Tynan dropped to one knee and stared into the blackness of the jungle. He strained his ears but could hear
nothing other than the hammering of his blood in his
head.

"How many?"

"Can't tell. They're off to the right, between us and
the river."

Tynan wanted to swear, but didn't. Instead, his mind
raced. The thing to do was divert to the left, up on the
side of the ridgeline, and try to avoid the enemy behind
them. That would move them in the wrong direction, but

Charlie would figure they would try to get to the river. If they pulled it off, then the V.C. who had been guarding the prisoners might think they escaped to the west and not the east.

"Skipper?"

Tynan waved at him, telling him to shut up. He kept his attention focused on the jungle, looking and listening, but still couldn't see or hear anything.

"You sure they're out there?"

"Yes, sir."

Tynan wiped a hand over his face. He turned and looked over his shoulder, thinking about the claymores they had planted along their route of retreat. If they left them in place, the V.C. were bound to trip them. The question was what the enemy would think. Would he believe that they had planted them coming in, or going out? Would it give them a clue about their route of travel? Would it be safer to pull them out?

"Callahan, I want you and Mathis to collect the claymores and booby traps we laid. When you've finished, follow us to the north up onto the side of the ridge. We'll try to avoid the enemy."

The other man didn't say a word, simply nodded his understanding. Tynan hoped they knew why he wanted them to pick up the booby traps. As Callahan and Mathis started out, Tynan pointed to the north and signaled for Jones to take point.

They fanned out in the jungle, Jones leading the way, with James and Tynan helping the two Americans. Neither of the prisoners had said a word since Tynan had appeared. They knew that the escape wasn't successful yet and that the enemy could discover they were missing at any moment. They could still be recaptured.

They had gotten two or three hundred meters from the V.C. camp when there was a single shout—a voice screaming one word in Vietnamese. In the quiet of the night jungle, Tynan could hear the commotion in the enemy camp that the shout caused. The men were coming awake and beating the bush, looking for the escaped men.

Tynan caught James and said, "You go ahead here. Watch the men. Wait until dawn about a click from here. If the rest of us don't show, head back to the east and loop in toward the river."

"Aye, aye, sir."

As James and the two prisoners headed toward the ridgeline, Tynan turned back toward the enemy camp. He moved rapidly now, making some noise but not enough to give himself away. As he approached the enemy, there was a single shot followed by a long burst from an AK. It sounded like one of the V.C. held the trigger down and burned through the whole magazine. Tynan saw neither the muzzle flashes nor the tracers.

He stopped when the firing broke out. Now there was more shouting inside the enemy camp. A light flashed and went out immediately. The shouting died out and there was another burst of automatic weapons fire. Monkeys overhead, shaken from sleep by the noise, shrieked in panic, rattling the treetops as they tried to flee.

Tynan hit the dirt, rolling to his right until he was next to the trunk of a tree. He watched the enemy camp, but the firing became sporatic and finally faded away. As quiet descended over the area, he caught sight of Callahan near by.

"We need to liven things up," whispered Callahan.

Tynan felt a grin spreading across his face. He could think of two ideas that had some merit and he liked them both. Two ways to liven things up.

"All right," he said. "Let's lob a couple of grenades into the middle of their perimeter to shake them up. You have a fix on the location of the enemy patrol?"

"Not exact," said Callahan.

"It strikes me that if we can get the two sides shooting at each other, the confusion will give us plenty of time to get the hell out of here."

He turned then and told Mathis to set the claymores again, two pointing at the enemy camp, and two pointing toward the enemy force behind them. He wanted a corridor between the two forces and the claymores, so that an attack from either side could be halted, if only for a few minutes.

Not waiting for a response from either man, he tapped Callahan on the shoulder and they began crawling through the jungle, more or less toward the river, so that they would be between the two enemy forces. He listened to the sounds that were beginning to come from the enemy camp. He stopped once and got to his knees, but could see nothing over the tops of the bushes. The enemy didn't seem interested in pursuing them—not at the moment, anyway.

Finally Tynan decided he had gone far enough. He touched Callahan on the shoulder and put his lips next to the other man's ear.

"I want us to stand and toss grenades in both directions. Two each. Once you've thrown yours, hit the ground until they detonate. Questions?"

Callahan didn't have any. He slowly got to his feet, as did Tynan. The two men stood back to back and jerked the pins free from their weapons. Tynan hesitated and then whispered, "Now."

Behind him, Tynan could feel Callahan turn slightly to throw his grenade. As he felt that, Tynan did the same, heaving the two weapons as far as he could throw them. He dropped to the ground and waited.

There were two crashing explosions from the enemy camp, and two in the jungle not far away.

For an instant everything was quiet as if the enemy soldiers were stunned. And then the jungle exploded. Firing broke out all around them. AKs hammered and were joined by a couple of RPD machine guns. Green-and-white tracers danced through the night, slamming into the trees and bouncing into the sky. The muzzle flashes of the weapons lit the landscape like the strobes from a dozen cameras. There was shouting and screaming.

"Jesus!" said Callahan, his voice sounding unnaturally loud after the explosions.

Tynan touched him again and whispered. "Use your weapon." Without another word, Tynan got to his knees and held his CAR-15 over his head at arm's length. He pulled the trigger, spraying the rounds around the jungle. He knew that the enemy would be able to tell the difference between their AKs and the Americans' CAR-15 and M16.

Callahan did the same, hosing down the suspected the enemy position. As they both emptied the magazines, they dropped flat and let the two sides shoot it out. The bullets snapped overhead, cutting through the leaves or punching into the trees. Bits of leaf and bark rained down on them.

"I think it's time to retreat," Tynan said almost conversationally.

"Thought you'd never come to that conclusion."

"Let's get out of here." Tynan began crawling to the rear. He moved rapidly, figuring that the little noise he was making would be lost in the sounds of the firing and maneuvering that the two enemy units were doing.

They found Mathis lying under a bush, the firing controls of the claymores clutched in his hands. As Tynan approached, he asked, "You want me to pick up the claymores?"

"No. Unroll the cables as far as you can and we'll punch them off."

Mathis did as he was told. They worked their way back, keeping their attention focused on the firefight developing between the two enemy forces.

When they reached the end of the cable, only about a hundred feet or so from the point where the claymores were set, they stopped. Mathis crouched with his hand on the controls but didn't fire them.

"You sure this is a good idea?"

"It'll add more confusion to the mess," Tynan said.

"But we probably won't get anyone."

"It'll draw their attention to an area away from us. That's all that matters."

Mathis shrugged and checked the controls one last time. He realized that he was delaying, waiting for the enemy to walk into the trap. But the claymores were hidden by the jungle and the darkness, so that even if the V.C. were crawling toward them, he would never see it. All he could do was punch them off.

Before he did, he glanced at Tynan a final time as if wanting confirmation. When Tynan didn't say anything, Mathis fired the claymores.

Tynan saw the flashes as the C-4 detonated and heard the steel ball bearings rip through the jungle. There were a few shrieks of pain and Tynan knew that they had hit a couple of the enemy.

The firing from the enemy positions increased, punctuated by explosions from grenades. Tracers whipped through the trees. There were shouting and bugles and whistles. It sounded like an NVA regiment was attacking.

Tynan couldn't help grinning. The plan had worked perfectly. He had two units of V.C. and NVA firing into each other, tossing grenades and shooting machine guns. It was a pitched battle without either side knowing what in the hell was going on.

Tynan touched the shoulders of both Mathis and Callahan. He leaned close, but still almost had to yell over the sound of the firing. "Let's get the hell out of here."

"Aye, aye, Skipper," said Callahan, his teeth barely visible in the darkness. It was the only thing visible about him. "I thought you'd never say that."

10

With the enemy fighting it out amongst themselves, Tynan and the two men with him were able to make good time through the jungle. They were on their feet, nearly running because the noise they made was overwhelmed by all the shooting. After five minutes it began to taper off. A few more Chicom greandes were thrown by the Vietcong.

As the shooting ended, Tynan slowed down. He stood for a moment listening, but there were no signs of pursuit. Both the enemy units were probably trying to break contact, figuring that the rising sun would give the other side an advantage. Tynan checked the time and found that sunrise wasn't that far off. He stopped long enough to relay the information to Callahan and Mathis. Then they started again.

They climbed the side of the ridge, stopping short of the summit and then turning to the east. Now, with the shooting ended, they were moving slowly again. They crept along, their feet cushioned by the rotting vegetation underneath them. They ducked under branches and around trees, avoiding contact with the vines and the ferns. They didn't want to give the enemy a trail to follow, if the enemy could get organized enough to search for one.

After thirty minutes, Tynan stopped to rest, Callahan and Mathis taking cover near him. He leaned against the smooth trunk of a teak tree, his forehead on his arm, gulping the air and feeling the sweat drip. Now it was going to get very interesting. He had to quickly find Jones and James and the freed prisoners and put more distance between them and the enemy. And he had to do it in the dark, without making a great deal of noise.

It was then that he remembered the packs. Tynan had ordered them left behind, figuring they could get to them, and now couldn't. The food, the main radio, the spare ammo and the other equipment was in the jungle to the east and south of where they were. That severely limited their options. Every time Tynan tried to second-guess the enemy he failed. If he'd known about the second unit, he'd have taken the packs with him.

But now wasn't the time to worry about it. He needed to get the team back together. Crouched near the foot of the tree, he listened, but there was nothing to give him a clue. He glanced to the rear, where Callahan and Mathis waiting. Tynan nodded and began moving again, hopefully heading in the direction of Jones and James.

It didn't take him long to find them—or rather, for them to find him. There was a hiss to his right and Tynan froze. He crouched, his finger on the trigger of his CAR-15, and then said, "Jones?"

"Skipper."

Tynan moved toward the sound of the voice. He found Jones and knelt next to him.

"Got a problem, Skipper."

"Only one?" Tynan thought that it would be one of the men they had freed, but that wasn't the case.

"There's another group in here. I counted ten of them, situated between us and the river. No way for us to get to our gear."

"Shit," hissed Tynan. "You mean other than the second group following the first?"

"Seems that way. They've taken up a position on the valley floor like they're setting up as a blocking force behind us."

Tynan glanced at the ground and realized that he could see it better now. It was getting lighter in the jungle, which meant it was very close to sunup. In fifteen minutes it would be easy to see. He had to act quickly.

They could retreat up the slope and over the top of the ridge: that would put the hill between them and the enemy they knew about, but it also put the hill between them and the river, where rescue was only minutes away. With the jungle as thick as it was, there wasn't much chance that they could signal a chopper from the ground even if they could find an LZ large enough for a chopper to use. And anything they did to get a chopper would alert the enemy as to their location. They needed to either get a radio or reach the river.

He wiped a hand over his face and rubbed it on the sweat-soaked, rotting fatigues. Now he wished that he'd let Mathis retrieve the claymores rather than punch them off—another lousy decision. He'd have to start making good ones or they were all going to be in trouble.

"How are the prisoners holding up?"

"Physically they're in fairly bad shape. We need to get them medical treatment soon but I think we can count on them for a day or so."

"You find out who they are?"

"Wanted to ask, but didn't want to discuss it in the jungle with the bad guys all around us. Thought it would be better to let it go for now."

"Let's join them and then we'll figure out what to do from there."

"Aye, aye, Skipper. Follow me."

They worked their way down the hillside toward a large clump of bamboo and ferns. He stopped short and then entered it with Tynan and the others right behind him. Once they were inside, Tynan pointed for the men to take up defensive positions.

He collapsed to the ground and tried to think. They could stay where they were through the heat of the day, letting the enemy search for them, if the enemy was inclined to do that. The fact that the prisoners were missing and there were V.C. dead would indicate that something was going on, so the enemy would probably search, if only to get revenge.

Lying among the bamboo and the ferns would not ensure their not being discovered. If the enemy found them, Tynan didn't think they could shoot their way clear. At least, not keeping everyone alive; not with two Americans who were not in very good shape. Without the two men, the SEALS could probably slip away with very little difficulty.

The best course was to get the men moving to the east and then turn back to the river. But first he had to get them moving. Quickly. He turned and got to his feet. He found Jones and leaned close to him.

"Dave, we've got to get out of here. We stay here, we're going to get caught and shot to hell. I want you on point."

"Aye, aye, sir."

"Give me ten minutes to brief the others and then head out. Keep it slow and quiet. Move first to the east and then turn back to the river."

Jones nodded his understanding. Tynan worked his way around the perimeter, talking to his team. He stopped long enough to look at the freed prisoners. One wore black pajamas like the V.C. while the other was in the rotting remains of his fatigue uniform. Both looked tired and they both looked sick. Their skin color was bad and the flesh hung on their bones from not eating properly. But the

eyes were bright and full of life. Tynan knew that both
would be able to keep up for a short period of time,
maybe only a couple of hours or maybe for a day, but he
couldn't count on them for very long. They would be too
weak from improper diet, lack of medical treatment, and
any diseases they might have picked up.

There were so many questions that Tynan wanted to
ask them, but there wasn't time. They had to get moving
and they didn't need a long conversation about the con-
ditions of their imprisonment, no matter how curious he
was.

He found Mathis and said, "I want you to stick with
the men and protect them. That's your job. You find them
lagging back, unable to keep up, you let me know."

Mathis nodded.

He briefed the other men on how he wanted them positioned. There would be a point, two flankers guarding
the center element of Mathis and the two Americans, and
then a rear guard. Tynan hoped that if anyone ran into
trouble, it would be one of the elements away from the
center. That would give Mathis the opportunity to get the
prisoners out of the way of danger.

Jones moved out then, disappearing into the jungle
growth. He had one of the intersquad radios and, once he
was outside the defensive area, used it to tell Tynan that
it was all clear to the east.

With that, they all began to creep through the jungle.
They didn't move fast, trying to be as quiet as possible.
Tynan let the men get out in front of him and then began
to follow. He listened to the jungle around him, but heard
only the animals and the insects. If the Vietcong were
searching for them, they were doing it very slowly and
very quietly.

He forgot about the heat and the humidity, which began their steady increase with the rising sun. He ignored

the discomfort and kept moving. He refused to think about the sleep he hadn't gotten or the Dexedrine that he had taken. All he wanted was to get through the jungle without running into any more of the enemy.

And then, just as he was beginning to think they had skirted the blocking force that had been in the way, the radio snapped, letting him know that the enemy was on the move. Tynan halted, listened, and then eased under a bush to hide.

At first, he heard nothing in the jungle around him. Then there was a quiet snap as a twig broke and Tynan saw one of the enemy freeze. He glanced right and left, apparently wondering if anyone had heard him. When he decided that no one had, he began to move again. But he changed had direction and was now heading straight for Tynan.

There was nothing the lieutenant could do. If he moved at all, the V.C. was sure to see him. He was trapped. The enemy soldier came toward him, stopping once to poke his rifle barrel into a bush, and then turned as he neared Tynan.

Tynan realized that he had made a mistake. If the enemy soldier found him, Tynan was in no position to fight back. He had to get free and hope that the V.C. didn't see him. If he did, Tynan had to be in a position to kill him quickly and quietly because to shoot him would bring the whole enemy patrol down on him.

Without waiting to see how good the V.C. was, Tynan started to work his way to the rear, away from the enemy soldier. He pushed himself from under the bush, keeping it between him and the Vietcong, and crouched behind the bush. The V.C. was now only a shadow, still coming toward him.

Tynan set his weapon on the ground at his feet, the operating rod up to keep it out of the dirt. Slowly he reached up and drew his knife. As it came from the scabbard, he crouched forward, on the balls of his feet, ready to spring at the Vietcong.

It seemed that the man was drawn toward Tynan by some unseen force. He walked straight toward him, stopping long enough to poke the bush, and then moved around it. He stepped right up to Tynan as if he didn't see him and then froze.

Tynan didn't hesitate. He grabbed the barrel of the man's rifle, jerking him forward. Rather than letting him pull the trigger, Tynan yanked upward, breaking the Vietcong's finger. The man whistled through his nose in sudden pain and released his weapon. Tynan dropped it to the ground and snagged the front of the enemy's shirt, pulling him closer. As the man fought to keep his balance, Tynan slashed with his knife, cutting the man's throat. His blood spurted, soaking Tynan and wrapping him in the smell of hot blood.

The man sagged in Tynan's grip and Tynan lowered him to the ground. As he did, he heard a noise to his right and dived to the left. He rolled once and snatched up his weapon. There was a burst of AK fire that crashed into the ground near him. The rotting vegetation and muddy ground splashed around him. He rocked to the right and jerked the trigger of his own weapon, firing twice.

The enemy soldier took both rounds in the chest, staggering back as the blood blossomed on his uniform. He tried to raise his AK but no longer had the strength. As he dropped it to the ground, he turned to the left and fell into the jungle with a crash.

Over the radio, Tynan heard, "Say status."

Tynan whispered back, "Rear guard in contact. Keep moving and get clear."

There was another burst, this one from farther away, and poorly aimed. Tynan didn't even hear the rounds. He searched for the enemy soldier, but couldn't see him. Tynan moved farther to the rear, away from the rest of his men. He stopped and listened, and then started out again, trying to draw the enemy away from the rest of the team.

Finally he turned, heading toward the river. After several minutes he stopped and listened. Somewhere in the jungle to his left he heard a man moving. The man was trying to be quiet, but was making a slight rustling sound. The solution to the problem was a grenade, but Tynan wasn't sure where his own men were. He couldn't throw his grenade until he identified the target. He wasn't going to make the mistake that the V.C. and NVA had made the night before.

He settled down, nestling against the trunk of a huge tree. He leaned back against it and searched the jungle. There was movement in the trees over him. Monkeys chattering and running through the canopy. It was a distraction that Tynan didn't need or want.

Then in the distance, he caught a flash of movement. Just a blackness against the deep dark green of the jungle. Using his peripheral vision, Tynan spotted the enemy soldier who was now no more than twenty or thirty feet away—a young man who wore the khaki of the NVA and carried an AK-47.

Tynan slipped around the trunk of the tree and raised his own weapon. He sighted quickly, aiming at the man's head since he couldn't see his chest. As he squeezed the trigger, he realized that he was giving away his position but he didn't care. It would draw the enemy toward him and away from the others, giving them a chance to get away.

The weapon fired and he saw the man's head explode in a spray of crimson and green-gray. The soldier threw his weapon into the air and disappeared from sight.

As he did, Tynan was moving again, away from his tree. There was a rippling of enemy fire. Some of it tore into the thick trees and some of it passed overhead. Tynan dropped to the dirt, crawling rapidly deeper into the jungle, away from the rest of his men.

He heard what sounded like a rock thrown through the top of a tree. Tynan knew that it was a grenade. Off to the right was a dull thud as the low-power Chicom weapon exploded. The shrapnel ripped through the bush over his head and he caught a whiff of cordite.

He rolled to the left and got to his knees. Crouching over, he ran through the jungle and leaped over a fallen log. He dropped to the ground and crawled back to it. He poked the barrel of his weapon over the top and wondered just what in the hell he had gotten himself into. Alone in the jungle with a radio of limited range, no food, and only one canteen that had any water in it.

But then, before he had a chance to dwell on it, there was more movement around him. He ducked down, pressing his face against the side of the log, and inhaled deeply. He smelled the wet, moist dirt and the rotting wood. As he glanced up again, he saw two men in black pajamas working their way toward the position he had occupied earlier.

Instead of shooting, he set his rifle down, with its barrel propped against the log. As he rolled to his back, he grabbed a grenade and pulled the pin. He shifted around until he could peek over the top of the log: both of the enemy soldiers had stopped moving and seemed to be waiting for Tynan to do something so they could find him.

He arched his back and threw the grenade as hard as he could. He felt the muscles in his arm snap as he released the weapon and realized that he wouldn't be pitching in the World Series.

The grenade landed near the feet of one of the men. He stared at it in horror and then reached down for it. Just as his fingers touched it, there was an explosion. Tynan lost sight of the men in the fountain of dirt and debris that shot into the air. As it cascaded to the ground, he snatched his rifle. When the air cleared he could see the bloody body of one man. The other seemed to have vanished in the explosion but Tynan was sure he was dead.

For a moment it was quiet. Then a machine gun opened fire. Tynan couldn't spot it but at first could hear the bullets from it. As he turned, there was a snapping over his head as the rounds ripped through the jungle. He knew that the gunner was trying to draw fire so that the enemy could find him. Tynan wasn't dumb enough to fall for that old trick.

Instead, he slipped to the rear, away from the log and the enemy forces. He kept his head down, sliding around one bush. He got to his knees and then to his feet, keeping his eyes moving, but now there was nothing to see. The only noise, except for the sporadic hammering of the machine gun, was the shrieking of the monkeys in the trees.

There was a crashing beside him and Tynan spun toward it as one of the V.C. leaped at him. He ducked under the man like a quarterback shedding a blitzing linebacker. But instead of ducking completely under the man, Tynan lifted a shoulder, throwing the enemy to the ground. He dropped his full weight on the man's chest, his right knee smashing the breastbone. Over the sounds around him, Tynan heard the bones snapping. The enemy convulsed, swinging his arms and kicking his legs as the breath was crushed from him.

As the man died, Tynan rolled away from the body. He came to his hands and knees and listened carefully. The machine gun had stopped firing and the jungle was quiet. Tynan got to his feet and drifted to the rear. He held his rifle in both hands, a finger on the trigger.

Again he heard a noise to the right. He slipped to one knee, his shoulder against the rough bark of a tree. He aimed at the sound, but didn't shoot. The logical thing was to use a grenade, but he only had two left. He didn't want to waste them on an unidentified noise in the jungle.

He kept his eyes fastened onto the patch of jungle where he had heard the noise. There was a shadowy movement and Tynan waited. A moment later a man appeared—but it wasn't one of the Vietcong. Tynan grinned and began to work his way toward the man.

When he was close he whispered, "What in the hell are you doing here?"

Mathis dropped and whirled, his weapon coming around, but he didn't fire. He breathed a quiet sigh of relief and said, "Looking for you. Heard the shooting and thought that you could use the help."

Tynan nodded and pointed to the rear. "I think the equipment is stashed over there. We need to get to the radio."

Mathis nodded his understanding. He turned again, his weapon at the ready. Tynan stepped in front of him and began to glide through the jungle. He walked slowly, quietly. He ducked once but the motion he'd seen had been a monkey near the ground.

Tynan looked back and then stopped. He thought that he recognized the jungle. He was near the place where they had hidden the day before.

He leaned close to Mathis and said, "A couple of minutes and we'll be at the radio."

Mathis nodded.

Tynan started to move again. He stepped over a lacy fern and then the trunk of a fallen tree. He thought that he could see the clump of bushes and trees where they had concealed their equipment before the attack.

"Okay," whispered Tynan. "Let's get our shit and get the hell out of here."

Mathis crouched down and stared into the glowing green of the jungle. He nodded again, but there was tension on his face. The exertion of having to move quietly and the oppressive heat of the jungle were beginning to get to him.

Tynan stepped forward and froze, staring for a moment before he backed up. He touched Mathis on the shoulder, nodding toward the rear. They retreated several meters until they were under cover near a clump of trees surrounded by flowering bushes.

"What is it?" asked Mathis.

Tynan shook his head and leaned close. "There's a patrol sitting on the top of our equipment."

"Do we get out now?"

"No. We figure out what to do and go get it. We need that damned radio."

11

"It shouldn't be that difficult," whispered Tynan. "Only four of them in the way."

Mathis didn't look like he believed it was going to be as easy as Tynan thought it would be. But he nodded his agreement, slung his weapon, and pulled his knife from the scabbard.

"This is going to take real coordination. We've got to take four guys at once with only two of us to do it."

Tynan then told Mathis that he wanted them to work their way closer to the enemy. If one of them was isolated in any way, he would be taken out. If they could do it quietly and quickly, they might be able to pull it off. If not, they would open fire and shoot the enemy. Tynan hoped they could get to the radio and get out before the enemy had a chance to mount any kind of a counterattack.

"Not much of a plan."

"No, but it's the best I have unless you've got a couple of ideas that I don't know about."

"No, sir."

"Then let's get at it."

Tynan led the way, creeping through the jungle. He watched the enemy when he could see them, moving when they looked away and stopping when they seemed to be staring at him. It was slow, nerve-wracking work.

At any moment one of the V.C. could sight something
and open fire. But then Tynan took cover in the ferns and
bushes at the edge of the trees where the equipment was
hidden.

He stopped then, resting for a moment. Listening, he
heard a quiet conversation in Vietnamese. He glanced to
the rear and signaled Mathis to the right, himself contin-
uing on to the left. He got to his belly and crawled forward, being very careful where he put his hands, knees,
and feet.

One of the V.C. broke from the group and started toward him. Tynan froze and then saw the man grabbing at
his crotch. He was going to relieve himself. He had left
his weapon and his helmet with the other men. It was a
perfect situation.

The man moved to the opposite side of a bush and
squatted there with his eyes closed.

Tynan hesitated before he struck. There were so few
real pleasures available to men in the jungle, and the man
was indulging in one of them. He hadn't shown very good
sense in leaving the others when it was known that an
armed enemy was in the area.

The man finished and grabbed a handful of leaves. As
he did, Tynan leaped. He grabbed the man under the chin
and jerked him to the rear. As they both dropped to the
ground, Tynan used his knife to slash the man's throat.
A gout of blood covered Tynan's hand, and as the man
kicked out, Tynan plunged the knife into his chest. The
blade penetrated the heart. The man went rigid and then
limp and then he died.

Tynan rolled the body off him and slipped to the rear,
away from the dead man. There was a sudden shout and
then a shot. Tynan didn't hear the bullet hit.

He got to his feet, grabbing at his weapon, and whipped it around, but there was nothing to see. He dodged to the left and crouched near a large tree.

The shooting increased. First there were AKs—one firing single shot and then a second firing on full auto. It was answered by an M16. There were two well-spaced shots.

Tynan got to his feet and ran to the south, stopping to take cover between two tall trees. Through gaps in the vegetation, he could see two of the enemy soldiers. He raised his weapon to aim when Mathis leaped into view. Mathis shot one of the men in the head. He dropped in a loose-boned fashion that meant he was dead. Blood spurted once as the heart contracted a final time.

The second man turned and fired at Mathis, but the round was wild. Mathis kicked out, knocking the weapon from the enemy's hand. The man jumped toward Mathis, but the SEAL fired once driving him back. The V.C. collapsed to the ground and rolled to his side. Mathis looked up, almost as if he knew where Tynan was standing.

There was a burst from the rear. Mathis jerked upright, dropped his weapon, and touched his chest. He fell forward, landing on the body of the dead V.C. As he fell, the last of the enemy soldiers appeared, his weapon pointed at Mathis's body.

The Vietcong crouched over Mathis. He put his weapon down and began to pull at the Mathis's pockets. When he found nothing in them, he tried to unbuckle the pistol belt.

Tynan couldn't stand that. It was one thing that he had never seen before. In the past, he had searched the bodies of the enemy dead, taking documents, orders, wallets, pictures, and a lot of other things. But he had never been around to watch the enemy do it to someone he knew.

The V.C. tried to roll the body over. He had his back to Tynan. Tynan now moved forward. As he approached the man, he turned to look. Tynan kicked up like he was trying to make a fifty-yard field goal. The man's head snapped back as he flipped over with a groan. As he hit the ground, Tynan used his knife to finish him.

Tynan let the body slide to the ground, and then moved to look at Mathis. Blood covered his chest and his face was waxy, looking unreal. His unseeing eyes were staring into the canopy over him. There were still beads of sweat on his face and staining his underarms. If it hadn't been for the holes blown in his body, Tynan would have believed the man still lived.

A shout from the jungle snapped his attention back to the present. He dived for cover and lay there, listening. There was no way that he could get Mathis's body out of the jungle. There were too many enemy soldiers in the way and too much ground to cover. He crawled to it and pulled one of the grenades from it. He yanked out the pin and then shoved the grenade under Mathis so that the weight of his body held the safety spoon in place. When someone rolled the body over, the grenade would explode.

Then, in a fit of slyness, Tynan did the same for one of the dead Vietcong. Even if he killed and wounded some V.C.s with the grenade under Mathis, the enemy wouldn't expect their own dead to be booby-trapped. He might get a couple more that way.

When he had finished, he crawled away from the dead men, away from the smell of death and the odor of blood. Already the flies were beginning to swarm, following the rancid smell of dead meat in the hot tropical sun. Here in the jungle, bodies began to decay almost at the very instant of death.

Trying not to hear the flies, or smell the stench of death, Tynan searched the clump of trees until he located the stashed equipment. He pulled the radio and the spare batteries from the pile. He stared at it for a moment, wishing that there was something more to be done. The last thing he wanted was to leave useful equipment for the enemy.

Since his options were limited, Tynan used one of his remaining grenades to booby-trap the equipment in the same fashion that he had booby-trapped Mathis—a grenade with two cartons of C-rations on top of it to hold the safety spoon down. If someone picked up the C-rats, the grenade would go off. Tynan hoped that the explosion would ruin everything.

That finished, he had to get out. He looked at his watch, surprised that it was only midmorning. With everything that had happened, he was convinced that the day had to be about over. He took a deep breath and began crawling to the north, toward the ridge, where he hoped he could find the rest of the team. With all the shooting that had been going on, he wasn't sure that anyone would be handy.

Because the enemy was all over the area, he had to move slowly and carefully. He stopped once because he heard someone walking, but the sound faded and he never did see who it was. While he waited, he broke squelch twice on his short-range radio, but got nothing in response. That only meant that he wasn't within a hundred yards of his men or that he had pointed the antenna in the wrong direction.

When he was sure that the enemy soldier had moved on, Tynan began to crawl again. He stayed low, moving slowly and listening for the enemy. There were occasional shots from AK-47s but Tynan knew it was Charlie's attempt to draw fire so that he could locate the

Americans. No one returned it, meaning that his men were too far from the enemy to worry about them or too smart to fall for a recon by fire.

For twenty or thirty minutes he kept moving, crawling forward, stopping, and starting again. The shooting by the enemy became distant like the dull pops of artillery heard from miles away. At one point, he rested under a fallen tree. He sipped the last of the warm water from his canteen, drinking it all because he didn't want it sloshing around as he made his way back to his men.

Again he tried the radio, waving the antenna around but getting no response. Finally he decided that he had wasted enough time and slipped from his cover. Now he got to his feet but moved in a crouch, sliding from shadow to shadow and staying out of the small patches of sunlight that filtered through holes in the canopy.

He reached the slope leading to the top of the ridge. He assumed that he was now west of where he wanted to be and began to work his way to the east. He ranged up and down the slope, looking for a sign of anyone who might have passed by in the last few hours. He didn't care whether it was from his men or the enemy, as long as he found a trail.

Every so often he tried the short-range radio, hoping to establish contact with someone in his team. When that failed, he moved off again, working away from the enemy camp and location.

After a hour or more, he decided he had moved far enough to the east. Now he began a looping swing across the valley floor, heading in the direction of the river. He stopped to rest once, lying under the leaves of a fern that dripped water onto his face. He listened to the jungle but it had turned from a deadly environment filled with enemy soldiers to something that was almost friendly, providing him with water. The only sounds were the buzzing of the insects, the chattering of distant monkeys, and the calls of the birds. Sometimes he heard a jet that was invisible or the popping of helicopter rotors as it flew above the triple canopy.

Before he moved, he tried the radio again. He broke squelch a couple of times, waited, and tried again. He strained to hear and thought he detected a response. He sat up, pointed the antenna and tried again. This time he heard an answer that was louder than before.

Tynan tried again, whispering a quiet message. A second later there was a response from Jones. Tynan wanted to shout. He wanted to leap to his feet and run to Jones and the team. Instead, he said, "Give me a short count every five minutes."

Jones rogered and made the first count.

Since his equipment was directional in nature, he knew in which direction to move. Without haste, he moved from the hillside out onto the valley floor. He stepped carefully, not wanting to help the enemy if Charlie was around. He avoided muddy places on the ground and tried not to crush the small plants or break twigs on the large ones, moving through the jungle with the grace and eloquence of a light breeze.

Jones gave him another count and Tynan realized that he was moving too far west. He turned and continued, watching the jungle. On the next count, he knew that he had to be close to the team. He crouched, examining the vegetation around him. Finally, he caught a flash of something in the distance that didn't seem to belong and moved toward it. Within minutes he was standing over Jones, who was about to give another count.

Jones turned as the shadow fell on him and nearly jumped. He stared up at Tynan and mouthed the words: "You scared the shit out of me."

Tynan ignored that and knelt next to the younger man. "What's the status here?"

"We're ready to move. The two men have had a chance to rest and want out of here badly."

Tynan couldn't help but grin. "You get anything out of them?"

"Names and ranks. One's an army staff sergeant named Vincent Olfield and the other is a marine corporal named Bruce Blackburn. Olfield has been held for about nine months and Blackburn for nearly six. Olfield was captured in the delta and Blackburn up in I Corps."

"Christ, they move these guys around pretty good," said Tynan.

"Yes, sir. Where's Mathis?"

"Mathis didn't make it. Took out a bunch of them. I had to leave his body but I booby-trapped it." He waited for Jones to respond and when he didn't he added, "I also picked up the main radio."

"That's something."

Tynan checked the time and said, "I make it a five or six hours until dark. Seems to me that we should stay here until nightfall and then slowly work our way to the river. We'll have all night to get the four or five clicks."

"Our guys will be okay, but it might be a hardship on Olfield and Blackburn. It's hard enough moving through thick jungle in the day."

"The night will give us good cover. In the day, too many things can go wrong."

"Aye, aye, Skipper."

Tynan sat down and wiped the sweat from his face. Suddenly he wanted to talk. Talk about anything except the jungle and the mission. He wanted a chat in a cold room with a beer in his hand without having to worry about the relentless pressure of the jungle that hid enemy soldiers.

He physically shook himself and leaned closer to Jones. "Let's draw the team in and form a perimeter. I want everyone to get some rest. I think we'll be awake all night again."

Jones nodded and used his radio to call in the team. Tynan listened for them but couldn't hear them moving until Callahan, who had inherited Olfield and Blackburn, made his way over. The two men were weak from their months in captivity and made some noise. It wasn't much.

When the team was joined, Tynan used hand signals to spread them out and tell them what he wanted from them. They responded in kind, slipping into position so that the enemy wouldn't be able to sneak up on them. Tynan told every other man to take a break and catch some sleep if he could.

Tynan lay down on his stomach, facing north. He could see only ten or twelve feet in the thick jungle. But it wasn't his turn for guard duty so he tried to sleep, but the Dexedrine wouldn't let him. It kept rubbing his nerves raw. With it, he thought he could hear better and see better. The heightened senses picked up the tiniest sound and magnified it, making it impossible for Tynan to sleep. But he could at least rest.

He closed his eyes, listening to the jungle. He thought of times in Saigon and dreamed of cold beer, of women he knew and movies he'd seen—of anything but the jungle that surrounded him. He let his mind wander because he was supposed to be resting. Jones would let him know if anyone was coming. Jones would stay alert.

And then he felt Jones touch his shoulder. Tynan snapped his eyes open but Jones didn't have to tell him the problem: Vietcong were moving near them. He saw one man, an AK in his hands, slipping through the jungle. He was looking left and right but he didn't seem to be searching very hard. Once he stopped, stared up into a treetop, and then continued on. They could hear him moving long after he disappeared from sight.

When the enemy soldier was gone, Tynan took over the watch. He lay there quietly and let his eyes and ears do the work. Now he didn't think about cold beers and nights in Saigon. He concentrated on the task of spotting the enemy. He stayed with it until he noticed that the light was beginning to fade around him. It was time to prepare for the night march. He woke Jones and signaled him.

Jones awoke at once but said nothing. He took a drink from his canteen and offered it to Tynan. Tynan accepted it gratefully and drank deeply. He handed it back and then turned. He could see that the team was ready.

As soon as it was dark, the team formed up. They kept Olfield and Blackburn in the center, put out flankers and a point, but had no rear guard. Tynan didn't care, since they were getting the hell out. It would only be a few hours and they would all be out. Just a few hours.

12

Tynan, who had decided that he wanted to walk point, kept the pace slow. Just before they broke camp, he took another Dexedrine, and with the drug coursing through his veins, it was almost impossible not to hurry. He heard every sound, and even in the blackness of the triple-canopy jungle at night, he could see shadows and shapes flashing and flickering. There was a slight luminescence from the rotting vegetation. A light breeze rattling the branches and leaves covered the little noise they were making. But more important, the wind had gotten under the canopy and seemed to blow the humidity away so that the jungle had become more comfortable.

He stopped once when one of the flankers broke squelch on the radio, but the all-clear came almost immediately. He used the short break to check his compass, which glowed in the dark. The only thing was that it was so bright that it could destroy his night vision for several minutes. And because they were in dense jungle, it was nearly impossible to set a course on a distant object. He could see no distant objects.

After an hour, he called a halt with each man resting in place. Everyone was responsible for his own safety so no one could doze or eat. It was a rest period but not one of relaxation. While they crouched in the jungle, Tynan took another compass reading. His task wasn't that difficult because all he had to do was maintain a more or less straight path; that would take them to the river. He didn't care where they hit it as long as they *did* hit it.

When ten minutes were up, Tynan was on his feet again, moving to the river. He stepped carefully, trying to avoid snapping a twig or disturbing the carpet of rotting vegetation.

He knew that the enemy was around, they wouldn't have abandoned the search for the escaped prisoners as easily as that. But he could find no evidence of them. It might be that the search was concentrated elsewhere or it could be that the enemy was lying in ambush somewhere. Maybe they figured that the only real escape route was the river and had spread out along it waiting for the Americans to come to them.

That had to be it: the Vietcong had opted to put all their eggs in one basket. Using the radio, Tynan called another halt. As he crouched among the giant leafy ferns and near a clump of trees, he checked the compass for something to do. They had been moving in the right direction, but he didn't know how far they had traveled. He estimated the river was no more than a click or two away and wondered why he could detect no odor from it.

He pulled back the camouflage cover on his watch and checked the time. He would keep moving for another hour and then laager the team so that he could reconnoiter the riverbank. If the enemy was there, he should be able to spot them.

He signaled the all-clear and started the team forward again. Now he had them moving more slowly so that they made absolutely no noise. He nearly felt his way along with one hand out stretched like a blind man without a cane. He kept his eyes moving and his ears open, but saw and heard nothing that would suggest that the enemy was close.

Then, when he began to wonder if he had somehow lost his way in the dark, he caught the first whiff of the river. He signaled the men and they slipped to the ground, watching and waiting.

Tynan eased his way toward them, pulling away from the main body of the patrol. After several yards, he heard a quiet splash in the water and knew that the river was much closer than he had thought. He slid to the ground and began to crawl forward slowly, listening and watching.

The odor from the river became stronger. Tynan knew that he had to be almost on top of it, but couldn't see it. Finally he stood and spotted it through gaps in the vegetation, a long silver ribbon.

He dropped to the ground and worked his way to the bank. For a moment he hesitated, listening to the sounds of the insects and animals around him. They seemed natural enough but he knew that a well-disciplined ambush would blend into the surroundings so that the animal life wouldn't be disturbed by it. All he could do was check the bank.

He turned to his right and crawled along it, staying five or six meters from the edge. He stopped frequently, listening, but found nothing to suggest that the enemy had anticipated him. That could mean that Tynan and his men were farther east than the enemy thought, or that the enemy hadn't anticipated the move to the river. Maybe the V.C. thought it was too obvious a ploy.

When he was satisfied that the enemy wasn't lying in wait, he turned and worked his way back the other direction until he knew that the V.C. weren't there either, checking for nearly two hundred meters along the bank. That finished, he turned from the river and returned to his men.

Using the radio, he alerted them that he was coming in and then called them together for a final briefing. Face-to-face, sitting in a circle, Tynan told them that he thought it was clear all the way to the riverbank. They would work their way to it and then use the main radio to call in the riverboat. If everything worked out, they would be on the boat before daylight and by midmorning would be sitting in a bar in Saigon sucking down ice-cold beer.

For some reason he had expected a cheer with the good news, and then realized that this was not the place for it. The cheer would come when they were on the boat heading rapidly down the river.

"I'll take point," he said finally. "Flankers out no more than ten meters. Once we've reached the bank we'll spread out, one man facing the river and the rest watching the jungle. The V.C., if they attack, will not come from the water."

As he said it, he remembered a movie he had seen about World War II. The Germans had assumed that no one could scale the one side of their mountain fortress so they hadn't bothered to guard it. Naturally, it was the route that the Americans took, surprising the enemy. That was why Tynan had one man watching the water. He didn't expect the enemy from that direction, but it didn't mean they wouldn't come from it, if the V.C. were there to attack.

Once the men were settled and ready, Tynan pulled the main radio over and turned it on. He used the earpiece that reduced the noise from the speaker to an insectan buzz. He adjusted the gain knob until there was no static and raised the mike to his lips. Quietly he made the first of the calls.

He waited, heard nothing in return, and then made a second call. A moment later there was a response:

"Sioux Warrior, this is Sioux Warparty."

"Warparty, we are ready for pickup." Tynan wasn't sure exactly where they were, but suspected they were east of the place they had come ashore. "Be advised that we have moved, one to two klicks to the east."

"Understood, Warrior. We are inbound your location."

"Roger. Be advised that we have seen numerous Victor Charlies, but are not in contact with them."

"Roger. We are inbound your location. ETA in four zero minutes. Can you mark?"

"I have a strobe light."

"Roger strobe."

There was nothing more from the PBR. It had left its base, wherever that might be, and was coming up the river. All Tynan and his team had to do was sit tight until it arrived.

He snapped off the radio and checked the time. Then he settled down to wait. There wasn't anything more that he could do. The claymores had been used or lost. Most of the grenades were gone and he had little left in the way of ammo. If he had claymores, he would set them in a ring and pop them just before they tried to board the boat. It would keep the enemy away in those few critical minutes. With grenades, they could throw them, accomplishing the same thing though not quite as effectively.

That was, of course, if the enemy was around. The grenades wouldn't tip off the V.C.; the approaching PBR would do that. Tynan suddenly liked that solution. As the boat pulled in, each man would throw the last of his grenades to cover the retreat. It was perfect.

Now all he had to do was wait. Relax a little. Let the sweat evaporate from his face and body. Let the light breeze cool him, and inside an hour he would be on the deck of a PBR racing down river.

The signal from the short-range radio surprised him. He realized that one of his men was alerting him that someone was coming. He listened carefully and realized that six V.C. had taken up a position twelve to fourteen meters from the left flank of his line. Obviously the V.C. didn't know that Tynan and his men were at the riverbank.

Tynan told Callahan to stay put. When the PBR diverted to the bank, he was to throw his grenades at the enemy before retreating. Callahan acknowledged by breaking squelch twice, signaling "Roger."

Tynan waited twenty minutes and then tried to contact the PBR skipper by radio. He didn't seem bothered by the report and just rogered the message.

Again Tynan checked the time. He had wanted to draw in his line as the boat neared, but now was afraid that it would tip his hand. Instead, he left everyone where he was and made his way to the riverbank. He slipped down it until his feet were in the water. He froze there, strobe in one hand and rifle in the other, waiting for the PBR.

The first indication that a boat was coming was a low, distant rumble sounding like an empty dump truck on a gravel road. But the noise deepened and became unusually loud. He stared into the blackness until he caught a distant shadowy movement. He turned on the strobe, feeling like the biggest jerk in Southeast Asia because the strobe looked like the muzzle flashes of a weapon.

He made his last radio call telling the PBR skipper that he had them in sight. The skipper rogered and claimed that he saw the strobe.

As the PBR approached, the noise from the engine became a roar and the shape fragmented, confusing Tynan. Then he realized that there was more than one boat: Three at least, and maybe as many as four.

He used his short-range radio and said, "We go in three minutes. Grenades on my mark."

He watched as the boats grew in size as they neared him. He didn't want any one of them hanging around too long. Timing was critical. The V.C. that Callahan had spotted had to be wondering what was happening.

"Five," said Tynan. "Four. Three. Two. One. Mark."

When he spoke, he stood straight up and stepped farther into the river. He heard someone moving behind him and glanced up at the top of the bank. He recognized the shape of Blackburn, but he didn't turn to help him down. Instead, he pointed his strobe at the PBRs.

As he looked back up on the bank, he heard the first of the grenades detonate. A crash in the jungle, not far from him. A moment later came a second and then a third, which was followed by one tremendous, drawn-out explosion as several weapons seemed to detonate simultaneously.

"Yeah," he said.

Firing erupted in the jungle—AKs on full auto. Tynan saw some tracer rounds leave the jungle. There were ricochets and a few bounced off the water, tumbling upward.

The roar of the boats drowned out the noise then. One of them broke from the formation, its bow aimed right at Tynan. He stood there calmly, wondering if they were going to run him down.

The other PBRs raced by throwing up rooster tails of water in their wake. As they passed Tynan, their guns opened up, sending out bright yellow flashes and tongues of flame as they began hammering. Lines of ruby tracers tore into the jungle.

More of his men appeared on the bank above him. One of them helped Blackburn down into the water. As he reached it, the PBR turned and stopped about twelve feet from them. The bow wave washed over Tynan's waist, soaking him and his equipment, but he didn't care.

Tynan turned to watch the PBRs upriver. They seemed to have slowed and were pouring a steady stream of ruby-colored tracers into the jungle. There was a heavier, louder hammering as one of them opened fire with a fifty-caliber machine gun. The enemy shot back with AKs and one RPD, red tracers going in and green coming out. The orange and yellow flashes from the weapons gave the scene a Technicolor beauty.

There was a dull pop on the riverbank and shrapnel hit the water near him. Spinning, Tynan saw one of his men topple from the bank. He fell into the water with a splash and didn't move. Firing from M16s began above him. He could see his men outlined by the flashes.

"Let's go!" he called. "Move it! Move it!"

Jones appeared from the jungle, stopped at the top of the bank, and then jumped. He hit the water feet first and seemed to be moving before he landed.

"Right behind me," he warned. "Ten or twelve of them."

Tynan made a quick count. One man was missing now. He struggled through the water to the wounded soldier and found James floating facedown. He flipped him over and as he did, James choked once and threw up into the river.

The shooting seemed to grow in intensity. Bullets were hitting the water around them. Tynan dragged James into a sitting position but the wounded SEAL was only semiconscious.

Beside him, Jones crouched so that the water was nearly chest high. He was firing his weapon on full auto, hosing down the jungle and changing magazines as quickly as he could.

"We're missing one," yelled Tynan.

"Callahan hasn't made it out yet," said Jones. He didn't break the rhythm of his firing.

Tynan picked up James in fireman's carry and headed into deeper water. He heard bullets snapping through the air around him. He could see the splashes as they hit the water. There were *pings* as some of them slammed into the side of the boat.

Tynan reached the PBR and two hands loomed out of the dark. They snagged the belt and James was suddenly lighter. Tynan knew that someone on the boat was hauling the wounded man to the deck. As soon as his burden was gone, Tynan whirled.

He found Jones backing up, firing, firing, firing. He yelled at him, "We've got to get Callahan."

"If he's not here, he's dead."

Tynan wanted to believe that, because it meant he could crawl onto the boat and get out. But he needed to see the body to believe it. He could leave a body. Hell, who really cared about the body once the man was dead? But he couldn't leave a living, wounded SEAL. Not for the V.C. and NVA.

Without a word, he pushed past Jones, struggling for the bank. Firing behind him tapered and the engines on the PBR began to roar. The coxswain was telling him to get the hell out of the water or to be left.

Then, suddenly, there was a shape on the shore: a huge man holding an M16. He was silhouetted in the muzzle flashes, standing there, making his last stand. He was Horatio at the bridge and Davy Crockett at the Alamo. He was George Custer surrounded by all the Indians in the world. He held his weapon to his hip and his finger on the trigger. He was hunched forward as if fighting a stiff wind and he seemed to be screaming at the top of his voice.

Tynan couldn't see the enemy. They were hidden by the bank and the jungle and the darkness. He tried to run, but the slimy mud of the river bottom sucked at his feet, holding him tightly. He struggled forward.

He yelled, "We've got to get out. Now."

But Callahan didn't hear him, or ignored him, or perhaps didn't care anymore. He dropped the magazine from his weapon, slammed another home and began to shoot again. Green tracers from the enemy weapons swarmed around him like angry bees, but Callahan ignored those too.

Tynan reached the bank and grabbed at an exposed root to haul himself up. Behind him, the machine guns on the PBR began to shoot, adding to the din. There were explosions from grenades and a weird popping sound as a 40-mm grenade launcher started kicking out rounds.

Tynan tried to drag himself up, but the bank was slick. He slipped once and, as he fell to the water, he saw Callahan go down. The SEAL fired a burst into the sky as if to challenge the heavens. He rolled to his left and tried to get up, shoving the barrel of his weapon into the soft earth to use as a clutch. He was hit again and groaned in pain.

Tynan was now frozen, watching the drama unfold as if he were sitting in a theater. He reached out, his fingers clawing at the dark, but no one saw that.

Callahan managed to get to his feet. There was a wet slap, and he fell to his knees. He held his rifle in both hands over his head. As he began to fall to his face, he threw it into the river. A final act of defiance. One that would deny the enemy his weapon. A statement that said he would never surrender and that they could never defeat him.

As he threw the M16, he rolled over the bank and dropped into the water. Tynan turned and ran to him. He grabbed the front of his harness and hauled him up. Then, backing up, one hand on the pistol grip of his CAR-15, he dragged Callahan through the water.

The enemy charged forward, shouting and shooting, which only gave the men on the PBR clear targets. They raked the bank with a deadly fire from their weapons. Two of the enemy toppled into the river and the rest leaped for cover.

As the enemy firing ended, Tynan reached the boat. He lifted Callahan up and saw two of his men grab at the body. They pulled him onto the boat. Once Callahan was on board, Tynan tossed his CAR-15 up and grabbed the side. Others pulled at his arms, helping. Just as his feet cleared the water, the engine roared and the boat lurched. The coxswain spun the wheel, trying for the safety of the center of the river.

The other boats had also turned and were coming back downriver, pouring fire into the jungle on both sides. There was a single explosion in the trees. A fountain of sparks that burned out quickly.

Then they were away from the riverbank and the pickup point. The firing ceased. Tynan sat up and looked at his men. He saw Jones and said, "Status."

"Callahan's dead."

"Yeah, I kind of thought he was."

"James is wounded but it seems superficial. I think he hit his head when he fell. Blackburn and Olfield are okay. Neither of them were hurt."

"How about you?" asked Tynan.

"Nary a scratch, Skipper. Made it out in good shape."

Tynan got to his feet and looked out over the stern. The other boats were in a loose trail formation but no one was shooting now. He wiped a hand over his face and said, "Damn! We pulled it off."

"Not without losses," Jones reminded him.

"I know," said Tynan. "I'm sorry about that, but we did pull it off. That should be good for something."

Jones nodded.

Tynan took a deep breath and said, "Okay, let's get organized here. Jones, see if they've got a first aid kit to treat James and see if they've got some food to give to Blackburn and Olfield.

"Not wasting any time are you, Skipper?"

"Hell, man, you've had—what, five, six minutes off? What more could you want?"

"A cold beer."

Tynan had to laugh. Ask a sailor what he'd want and he'd tell you a cold beer or a woman. Tradition demanded that. To Jones, he said, "As soon as I can arrange for it, you'll have it."

"Thanks, Skipper."

Tynan left Jones and his men on the stern of the boat and stepped up to the coxswain. "How long before we hit the base?"

"Depends on what you want. We came off one that's about another twenty, thirty minutes away. You want a ride to Saigon, it'll be several hours."

"You realize that we've got a couple of men on board who were prisoners of war? Americans who were held as prisoners of war?"

The coxswain stared into Tynan's face. There was a dim red light coming off the instruments in front of him. He shook his head and said, "No, I didn't know that."

"Well, I'd like to get them into Saigon as quickly as possible. They may have some information that will help us find some other POWs."

"I understand," said the coxswain. "It'll piss off these other guys, but given the circumstances, I think we'd better push on to Saigon."

"I hoped you'd say that. Ah, you know, we don't need the other boats for an escort. They're released for their base. I'll be on the stern. Let me know when we get close."

"Sure." He glanced at his instruments and then added, "That was one hell of a pickup."

"That it was, Chief. That it was."

13

Naval Lieutenant Mark Tynan sat in the cool dim confines of a downtown Saigon bar with a beer sitting in front of him. He had spent the last five days being debriefed, sleeping, eating, and being debriefed again. He had provided oral reports and written reports. He had described what he had seen and then described what he believed he had seen. It had been a long, cruel process that was almost as bad as the days and nights in the bush. Now he wanted to relax, drink his beer, and wonder about where to buy a steak for dinner.

When a shadow fell across his table, he looked up, thinking that the waitress, dressed in a skimpy costume, had approached, but it was Commander Clafin.

"Mind if I join you?"

Tynan picked up his beer and sipped it so that he didn't have to speak. He kept his eyes on Clafin. Slowly, he set it down and said, "Last time I answered that question in the affirmative, I found myself ass-deep in the jungle surrounded by the entire North Vietnamese Army."

Clafin slipped into a chair and signaled the waitress. When he saw her coming his way, he said to Tynan, "Well, this time it'll be different."

"Uh-huh."

Clafin gave the waitress his order and then said,
"Thought maybe you'd like to know a few things that we
learned from the two men you freed."

"You going to tell me here, out in front of God and
everyone?" said Tynan, waving his hand to indicate the
bar and the Vietnamese waitresses.

"Only some of it. If you want the full story, you can
come in and read the official file."

The waitress returned, set a mixed drink in front of
Clafin. As she disappeared, Clafin added, "In the field I
would imagine that you didn't get a chance to talk to
either of the men for very long."

"Other than to learn their names and how long they'd
been held, I didn't talk to them. We found it advisable
to maintain noise discipline."

"Blackburn disappeared while walking point," said
Clafin without preamble. "It was one of those really
strange ones. Everyone assumed that he had been captured, but no one could figure out how they did it. Blackburn explained it."

Tynan nodded and waited. When Clafin didn't speak,
he said, "Well?"

"Oh, then you're interested?"

Tynan finished his beer and said, "Not if you're going
to keep handing it out piecemeal."

"Charlie used a tunnel system to get him. Situation apparently has to be set up just right, but when it is, they
can make people disappear. The point man or the rear
guard or flanker has to be out of sight of the rest of the
squad and the guy has to walk within a couple of feet of
the tunnel entrance. When the guy passes, they rise up
behind him, grab him, and drag him down into the tunnel. They slam the trapdoor and no one knows they're
there. Blackburn said that they hit him in the back of the

neck, stunning him. By the time he was conscious enough to realize what had happened, it was too late. His people had moved off in their search.''

"So we pass the information to the troops in the field," Tynan said.

"And they can make sure that the point men or whatever don't get too far away from the main body. Everyone keeps everyone else in sight, just as they're supposed to.

"We learned a couple of other interesting things from those guys. We've got a couple of teams in the field checking those out. Might turn something up.''

Tynan stared into the bottom of his empty glass. "You didn't come by here just to tell me that, did you?''

Clafin grinned. "You have a very suspicious nature.''

"With good reason.''

"Actually, I came by to pass down word from the admiral. He was quite pleased with the way you handled the whole thing. Even the somewhat unauthorized second mission. The results seem to be enough for now. Everyone is happy about them.''

"Pleased with the way I got two of my men killed?'' asked Tynan.

"You took on a couple of superior forces, inflicted heavy casualties on them and freed quite a few prisoners both South Vietnamese and American.''

"So I'll drink one to the memory of the men and thank the admiral for his faith in me.''

"Don't get sarcastic," said Clafin. "It was a fine job and you don't have to fish for more praise. The admiral is putting you and your men in for a decoration. He's pleased. You should be, too.''

Tynan stared at the man and wondered what he felt. Tynan knew that the deaths of his men bothered him, but it seemed that the navy couldn't care less. Tynan knew that the deaths weren't his fault, but he didn't want to get careless with the lives of his men. Not the way some officers did. But now wasn't the time to begin a long philosophical introspection. He could do that later, after he'd had time to put some distance between himself and the mission.

"So," he said, "the admiral was pleased?"

"Extremely. Said that he might have something for you in the future. Probably not in the same vein, but something that would take your special talents. Take someone who can think in the field and keep his mouth shut."

"Okay," said Tynan. "That sounds like a winner. Now, are you going to buy me a beer or do I have to leave?"

"I'll buy you one, and then I'll leave so that you can enjoy your days off."

"Thanks."

KILLSQUAD

by Frank Garrett

WANTED: A world strike force—the last hope of the free world—the ultimate solution to global terrorism!

THE WEAPON: Six desperate and deadly inmates from Death Row led by the invincible Hangman...

THE MISSION: To brutally destroy the terrorist spectre wherever and whenever it may appear...

KILLSQUAD #1 Counter Attack   75151-8/$2.50 US/$2.95 Can
America's most lethal killing machine unleashes its master plan to subdue the terrorquake planned by a maniacal extremist.

#2 Mission Revenge	75152-6/$2.50 US/$2.95 Can
#3 Lethal Assault	75153-4/$2.50 US/$3.50 Can
#4 The Judas Soldiers	75154-2/$2.50 US/$3.50 Can
#5 Blood Beach	75155-0/$2.50 US/$3.50 Can
#6 Body Count	75156-9/$2.50 US/$3.50 Can
#7 Polar Assault	75363-4/$2.50 US/$3.50 Can
#8 Slaughter Zone	75364-2/$2.50 US/$3.50 Can
#9 Devil's Island	75365-0/$2.75 US/$3.75 Can
#10 Mob War	75367-7/$2.75 US/$3.75 Can